RUBY KIND

PAUL PHILIP STUDER

This edition first published in paperback by
Michael Terence Publishing in 2024
www.mtp.agency

Copyright © 2024 Paul Philip Studer

Paul Philip Studer has asserted the right to be identified as
the author of this work in accordance with the
Copyright, Designs and Patents Act 1988

ISBN 9781800948976

No part of this publication may be reproduced, stored
in a retrieval system, or transmitted, in any form or
by any means, electronic, mechanical, photocopying,
recording or otherwise, without the prior
permission of the publisher

Cover image
Copyright © Luzina Valeriya
www.123rf.com

Cover design
Michael Terence Publishing
www.mtp.agency

Contents

MILLENIUM – THE YEAR 2000 1

THE BLITZ – 1940 LONDON 27

THE PLAGUE – 1576 VENICE 143

ALSO BY PAUL PHILIP STUDER 288

MILLENIUM

THE YEAR 2000

One

People were predicting the end of the world. Computers would crash, there would be massive power cuts, banks would collapse, planes would fall out of the sky, everything would grind to a halt.

Ruby's parents were sick with worry. They couldn't face seeing the New Year in. They took two sleeping tablets and went to bed early.

Ruby thought they were mad. She went to bed early herself and read her book. She was reading John Lennon's biography.

Nothing happened. It was a non-event. Everything carried on as normal. A lot of computer programmers made a lot of money out of people's fears.

Ruby switched on the television news and watched Sydney Harbour Bridge explode with fireworks, It was a spectacular sight. She was fifteen years old. In three weeks she would be sixteen. She was sitting her GCSEs this year. She was brilliant at music and art; in fact she was better than her teachers. If she had been at a private school, she would have sat her

Ruby Kind

GCSEs early and be taking A Levels this year, then onto university.

She was bored at school and had taken to bunking off and going into town.

Last Wednesday morning, she was walking down Coney Street in York, heading for WH Smith, the stationers. Her Gran usually bought her a token for her birthday. She hadn't decided whether to buy a CD or a book. She liked Robbie Williams' Millenium, but Mr Smales, the Art teacher had introduced her to Turner and Monet, the Impressionists and she wondered if Smiths had any books she could use as a reference. She normally borrowed books out of the library but you could only keep them for 3 weeks and she wanted to keep the art books.

In front of Smiths was a girl selling the Big Issue, a magazine that supported homeless people. It was cold, freezing, but the girl was only wearing a thin grey fleece, cheap dark blue tracksuit bottoms and tatty trainers. Her hair was long, dark, and greasy. Ruby wondered how old she was. She had dark smudges under her eyes, her cheeks were hollow and her hands were red raw with the cold. She could be anything from 20 to 40, thought Ruby. Ruby stepped in front of her and held out a pound coin, The girl grabbed it and gave her a magazine. Ruby didn't move. The girl hadn't looked at her. She kept her eyes on the ground

RUBY: 'Are you alright?'

GIRL: 'Feeling sorry for me, are ya, rich cow.'

Ruby didn't react. She reached into her pocket and brought out all the money she had, about five pounds. She placed the money in the girl's hand. She would have to walk home; she had just given away her bus fare.

Ruby started to move away. The girl grabbed her arm.

GIRL: 'Come on, I'll buy you a coffee. I can afford it now.'

The girl led the way to Starbucks, just round the corner. She ordered two cappuccinos and sat opposite Ruby at one of the little tables. Neither girl said anything, they just drank their coffee. The girl wrapped both hands round the cup for warmth as she drank. When she finished she looked Ruby in the eye for the first time and held out her hand. Ruby shook it.

GIRL: 'Yvonne.'

RUBY: 'Ruby.'

YVONNE: 'Don't be like me, Ruby. Make something of yourself.'

RUBY: 'What happened?'

YVONNE: 'It's a long story.'

RUBY: 'I've got all day.'

YVONNE: 'Shouldn't you be in school?'

RUBY: 'School's boring.'

Both girls had had the same thought: Ruby wanted to help Yvonne, and Yvonne wanted to help Ruby.

YVONNE: 'We can't stay here. They will chuck us out if we stop drinking. I know a place, come with me.'

Yvonne led Ruby down Coney Street and into St Martin le Grand Church.

YVONNE: 'Look around you. In a hundred years' time, this church will be a thousand years old. It is a hundred years older than York Minster. When this church was built, there was no electricity, no cars, no phones, life expectancy was 45. Kids were lucky if they saw their second birthday. A third of women died in childbirth. It was a totally different place, yet it's still here, still standing. Most people walk past and hardly notice it. They sat down on the back row of pews. Ruby was surprised when Yvonne took out a packet of cigarettes and lit one. She didn't think she should do that in a church, but they were the only ones there, so she didn't suppose it mattered.

YVONNE: 'It all started with these things.'

She blew out a long plume of smoke and looked at the cigarette.

YVONNE: 'I wish to God I had never seen the bloody things.'

She was quiet for a while, thinking. Ruby waited patiently. She wanted to hear Yvonne's story.

YVONNE: 'I was sat on the school bus when one of the boys produced a pack of cigarettes and passed them round. I took one. The boy, whose name was Bobby, lit it for me. He told me to inhale, which I did, and coughed my lungs out, we all did.

Over several weeks, we persevered until we were all experienced smokers. We had formed a sort of group, me, Bobby and two other boys. We took it in turns to buy the cigarettes and passed them round. My parents were reasonably well off, they gave me ten pound a week pocket money, but I needed more. So I got a job on Sunday at the

Farmers' Market. Strictly cash, no questions asked, no taxman, of course. I was 14 years old. Things went on like that for a while. I turned 15 and started studying for my GCSEs. The gang were sat on the bus, smoking as usual when Bobby said, 'I've got some weed, does anyone fancy trying it?'

The only weed I knew about was the weeds you pulled out of your garden, but no one in the gang wanted to show their ignorance. Bobby was the leader; we were all a bit in awe of him. We agreed to meet in Clancy's Wood, by the pond on Saturday morning, to try the mysterious weed.

The gang was sat round in a circle next to the pond. Bobby produced a large, white cigarette paper and started to fill it with what I thought was tobacco. He seemed to be piling plenty in. When he was satisfied, he licked one edge of the cigarette paper, and stuck it together to form a huge cigarette, six inches long by half an inch diameter. He called it a joint.

Bobby lit the joint, took a deep breath, closed his eyes, and inhaled. After a while he blew out a long plume of smoke. He seemed to be lost in his own world. Almost reluctantly, he passed the joint to the next boy. I was the last to have a smoke.

Paul Philip Studer

When we had finished the joint, Bobby collected five pounds off each of us and said he would get some more weed next week. Bobby's parents were old hippies; they liked to smoke a bit of pot now and then. They were careful not to overdo it though, they told themselves that they could control it. They were not drug addicts. They didn't realise that their son had crept down from his bedroom at midnight and watched them smoking a joint in the lounge. They were lost in a hallucinogenic state.

The gang became regulars in the wood. When the weather was bad, we all crammed into Bobby's Dad's shed. I had no idea where this shed was. When we went round to Bobby's house, there was no sign of the shed. Bobby made us put on blindfolds and hold hands. He led us over some grass and through a door. When we took off the blindfolds, we were in a little wooden shed with no windows, along each side were tall, spiky green plants. Above the plants were lights. It was surprisingly warm. I asked what type of plants they were. Bobby said they were a kind of South American lettuce, very good in salads. That's what Bobby's Dad had told him, but he knew better now, of course.

Ruby Kind

A few weeks later, I was reading in the press about a police raid on a cannabis factory in a house in Acomb. There was a picture of the plants. They were the same as Bobby's Dad's plants in his shed. I mentioned it to Bobby. He said: 'Yeah, well, keep it to yourself. We don't want the fuzz finding out.'

Bobby's brother, Simon, was a disc jockey. He was older, twenty three. He had travelled all over the country with his mobile disco. But last year, he met a girl in York and they had started going steady. The girl was called Anita and she didn't want Simon to be on the road all the time. So he went round all his usual clients and assembled a good list of references. Then he printed some fliers and sent them to every hotel, club, and firm that he could think of, within a 50 mile radius of York. He was astounded at the response. Within 6 months, he had 6 DJs working for him and he was still turning work down.

Three of the gang, including me, went on to the sixth form to do A levels. Bobby didn't bother. He went to work for his brother as a DJ. He was hoping he would make him a partner eventually. Simon thought Bobby was too young and inexperienced to do hotels and clubs, so he gave him mainly private parties to do. Bobby got the gang into as many of his parties as they wanted. We were averaging three a week – and we were taking Es at every one.

Obviously I fell behind on my school work, we all did. It got to six months before my A levels when I said to Bobby I was going to have to give up the parties and concentrate on my A levels. He totally understood. Then he offered me some cannabis 'just to help me relax', he said. Like a fool, I took it and stuffed it in my handbag.

I crammed and crammed and crammed, giving myself barely five hours sleep a night. I didn't do too bad, considering. I got a B and two Ds.

RUBY: 'What was the 'B' in?'

YVONNE: 'History, I love history. It's all around you, especially in York.'

RUBY: 'I thought so. It was the way you talked about the church. You made it come alive.'

YVONNE: 'Have you had enough? I told you it was a long story.'

RUBY: 'No, I'm hooked. It's like the best book I ever read.'

YVONNE: 'Except it's not a book, Ruby. It's real life. And it doesn't have a happy ending, don't ever forget that.'

Even Yvonne didn't realise though, how bad the ending would be.

They were quiet for a while. Ruby looked around the old church. It was quite narrow, with beautiful stained glass windows at the end and down the side. Big stone arches on the left. The roof was blue, with red and white coloured beams running across.

RUBY: 'You had just got a B and two Ds.'

YVONNE: 'Oh yes, well that was no good for the big universities, obviously. They wanted As, but I managed to get into Nottingham Trent University.'

RUBY: 'Studying history?'

YVONNE: 'That's right. I was determined to study quietly and get a good degree. I couldn't afford the Halls of Residence, so I answered an advert on the Student Union noticeboard for someone to share a house. It was a large run-down, terrace, with three boys, another girl and me. The rent was very low, so I took it.

All went well at first, until I noticed one of the boys was taking an interest in me. I had had boyfriends at school, of course, but they didn't last long. I soon got bored and chucked them. This lad was called Davey. He was a photographer and he was dead good looking. To be honest, I was a bit flattered that he was interested in me; all the girls fancied him.

We both had a free period one afternoon and we went back to the house and had sex. We couldn't do it any other time; there were too many people about.

Davey's nose was running. I said there was a handkerchief in my handbag. He searched round inside it and discovered the cannabis. I had forgotten all about it. He knew what it was. He said: 'Can we have a smoke?' I said yes, but not here. The smell is too obvious. We'll use one of the Student Union meting rooms. No one goes in them after 8 o'clock at night.' So we had a smoke. When we ran out of my stuff, Davey got some more.'

Two

'A lad on Davey's course was having a 21st birthday party. He was older than the others, having spent 3 years in South Africa working as a freelance photographer for little, local newspapers. He was a good photographer already, but he needed a formal qualification to get the job he wanted. His name was Ronan. He lived with his partner Mbeki in Beeston. They were renting a 3 bedroomed semi. Ronan never seemed to be short of money. Mbeki was a lovely black girl who was always smiling and laughing. Davey had already asked me to the party. I said I would have to see. I didn't want to get into the party scene again. Then Mbeki asked me to go so I couldn't say no.

I'm afraid I got rather drunk at the party. I hadn't let my hair down for ages and I was enjoying it. Davey whispered something in my ear and took me upstairs to one of the bedrooms. He shagged the living daylights out of me, first this position and then the next. I didn't know there were so many positions. He used two condoms; I guess he wore the first one out. When he had finally finished, I lay back on the pillow exhausted and he got up and reached inside his jacket pocket. He fetched out a square of silver paper, opened it and laid out two lines of white powder on the dressing table. He looked at me and said: 'Ladies first.' I asked him what it was, although I knew it was heroin. I said I wasn't sure. He said: 'Fair enough', blocked one of his nostrils with his finger, bent down and sniffed up one of the lines of white powder. He described what he was feeling.

DAVEY: 'It's amazing. It feels like everything is melting away and everything is better. I don't care anymore; nothing matters. I feel really floaty and nice. You need to try this, Yvonne. It's amazing.'

It sounded fantastic; I had to have a go. I sniffed the heroin the same as he had done and I felt pretty much the same. It WAS amazing.

I was hooked. I couldn't get enough of the stuff. Pretty soon I was injecting.'

Yvonne rolled up her sleeve and showed Ruby her arm. It was full of puncture marks.

'I failed my first year exams so badly that they kicked me off the course. Usually they give you a second chance and allow you to sit them again. I couldn't face going back home so I went to see

Ruby Kind

Bobby. He was very good. He got me into a squat at the White Swan Hotel in Piccadilly.'

RUBY: 'I know it; opposite Lloyds Bank.'

YVONNE: 'That's right. Bobby was their drug dealer. He got them anything they wanted. They welcomed me with open arms. Any friend of Bobby's was a friend of theirs, they said. That left me with the problem of money. They gave me food at the squat but they made it plain that I would have to pay my way. I also needed money for drugs. I signed on the dole, but that didn't go far. I needed a job.

I was wandering aimlessly around town when I found myself outside the Minster. I hadn't been in for years so I went inside and had a look around. A guide was showing a group around. I tagged on the back. When she had finished, I followed her back to the café. I had a little of my dole money left. When she asked for a coffee, I said: 'I'll pay for that.' She smiled and said: 'thank you.' I bought one for myself and we sat down at one of the tables. She was a middle-aged woman with a slight American accent. She wore a long black dress with a crucifix around her neck. She looked at me and said: 'What can I do for you, young lady?' I told her that I needed a job and I wondered how you become a

Minster Guide. I explained that I was a History student but I was taking a year off to look after my mother who had cancer. It was the first of many lies. I then told her everything I knew about York Minster and many other historical sites in the City. She was impressed. She sympathised with me about my mother and gave me a card. On it was written *'York Historical Tours'*. She told me her name was Maybelline and said to ring the number on the card and ask for Jack. 'Tell him I recommended you. With what you know, he should bite your hand off.'

I rang Jack and he invited me round to his house for an interview. I gave it everything I had. He sat back and said: 'I agree with Maybelline; when can you start?' I said anytime, I could work around looking after my mother.

Jack fetched a handout. He didn't put me in the Minster, he put me on the general York Tour. The handout contained all the historical information that I would need for the tour. He asked me how long it would take me to learn it. I said, 'about a week'. He said 'OK, I'll pencil you in for your first tour in two weeks' time. Come and see me when you are ready and I'll walk round the tour with you myself.

After we had walked round the tour, he said: 'I don't mind you adding the bits you said. In fact, make a few notes for me, would you. We may be able to organise another tour based on your knowledge.

I got the job. I walked back to the squat. I should have been happy; I had a job and somewhere to live. It was the best I could hope for, but there was only one thing on my mind: where could I find my next fix?

Somehow I managed to stay on an even keel and do the tours. Then I injected some bad stuff. I was smashed out of my mind for three days. I should have been in hospital but Bobby didn't want that. He was afraid that I might say something. No one likes bad stuff, especially the drug dealers. It damages their reputation. Bobby did his best to ensure his heroin was clean, but really he had no idea where it comes from. He just picked it up in a brown paper package from an old warehouse in Manchester, leaving a thousand pounds in its place. Getting bad stuff is a risk every drug addict takes. Bobby had never seen his supplier. He was just a voice on the end of a phone. Because drugs are an illegal substance, sold on the black market, they are not regulated, there is no quality control. You are at the mercy of ruthless criminal gangs and they don't give a toss about you. All they are interested in is making money.

Fortunately, one of the girls in the squat used to be a nurse. She looked after me, checked my temperature, pulse, blood pressure, tried to get fluids into me. Eventually I opened my eyes and asked where I was.

I had to get back to work, I needed money. I rang up Jack. Naturally he wanted to know where I had been. I said I had been rushed to hospital with an asthma attack, another lie. I had rung him as soon as I could. He asked me if I was alright. I said I was fine. I had my inhalers now and my little pink pills. I knew what to do if it happened again. He said he needed someone to do a tour next Monday and asked if that was too soon. I said I could manage it and that was that, I was back to work.

Then it happened again. This time, Jack sacked me. He had no choice. He had rung the hospital after the first time and found out that, of course, I had never been admitted to the hospital. He kept quiet about it. This time he said he knew that I had lied to him. He wanted to know what had really happened. I told him I was a drug addict. He said he had wondered about my mood swings. We were both silent for a while. Jack seemed to be thinking. He said: 'Is there anything I can do?' He is a good man.'

The sound of Queen's 'We are the Champions' rang out in the church. Yvonne pulled out a mobile phone from her pocket and pressed a button. Ruby was surprised she could afford one; she hadn't got one. Yvonne read her mind.

YVONNE: 'It's nicked. I keep getting text messages from a bird called Juliet. She's hot stuff. Look at that.'

Text message: 'Ring me darling. I am laid naked on the bed. I can't wait for you.'

RUBY: 'Wow! I see what you mean.'

YVONNE: 'I guess I've got Romeo's phone. I feel sorry for him. Look what he's missing.'

They laughed at that.

RUBY: 'What happened? You said Jack asked if he could do anything.'

YVONNE: 'He got me into a drug rehabilitation project. That's where I am now. They give me methadone. It's like a mild form of heroin, produces similar effects but not so high. I've been clean for 4 weeks. I think I'm going to be alright, Ruby. I may even go back to university eventually.'

RUBY: 'Good.'

YVONNE: 'Jack's even said he will keep my job open for me when I get better. Don't be like me Ruby. Learn from my mistakes. You don't need to experiment with drugs. I've told you what it's like. They destroy your life. I should be in my second year at university now, studying my beloved history. Instead, look at me. I look like a tramp. I'm just managing to crawl through every day, clinging onto the little bit of hope I've been given. Drugs are like a slippery slope. Once you get on it, it's difficult to get off. Even the so-called 'mild' ones are dangerous. It gives you an appetite for more. You have tasted the forbidden fruit. It's like an uncontrollable craving deep inside. Nothing else matters. Learn from me, Ruby. Make something of your life and don't you ever dare take any drugs or you'll have me to reckon with.'

Three

Ruby's parents were so caught up in their own lives that they didn't think she would want to do something special for her sixteenth birthday. They just gave her a hundred pounds inside her birthday card and told her to get something nice. Fortunately, not everyone was so indifferent.

At midnight, Ruby crept downstairs and out of the front door. She ran through the estate and onto the main Moor Road. A white Ford Transit van was parked by the bus stop waiting for her. Yvonne was stood by the back door of the van, smoking a cigarette. The two girls kissed each other and Ruby went round to the driver's door. The driver wound down his window and Ruby gave him a ten pound note. He reached in his pocket and pulled out a battered tin. He pressed a rubber stamp on it and stamped the back of Ruby's hand. Ruby looked at it. It was the outline of a butterfly.

Ruby and Yvonne climbed into the back of the van. It was crowded, there were no seats. Everyone sat on the floor. The driver turned the key in the ignition and the van moved off down Moor Lane. He didn't have far to go. He was headed for

Rufforth to an old show jumping arena. The owner made his money from car boot sales nowadays. It was more profitable than showjumping, but he used the arena for all sorts of things, including raves, which is what was happening tonight. The kids piled in from far and wide. Soon the place was heaving. The most important thing about rave music is the beat: constant, computer generated thump, thump, thump that never stops. No human drummer could produce such a beat. It never varied and could go on for ever. There was music as well and high pitched vocals, but the main thing was the beat. Strobe lights played over the dancers together with coloured spot lights. Everyone jumped up and down and waved their arms in the air.

A man was working his way through the crowd. He approached Ruby and Yvonne and offered them some white pills. Yvonne told him to piss off. When he persisted, she smacked him in the mouth. He got the message. Ruby didn't need drugs; she was high on adrenaline. She was having the time of her life.

Bobby had told Yvonne about the rave. He wasn't doing the disco himself; it wasn't his kind of music. But he said he would arrange transport for them if she liked. You just paid the driver ten pound for the entrance fee and the lift.

At 5 o'clock in the morning, someone switched off the music, turned on the main strip lights and opened the big roller shutter door to the kitchen. Bacon sandwiches, sausage sandwiches and mugs of tea were handed out. Ruby got back home at a quarter to six. She put her key in the front door and crept upstairs to her bedroom. She undressed, put on her nightie, and climbed into bed. Within five minutes she was fast asleep. The next thing she knew, her mother was shaking her shoulder.

AILEEN, RUBY'S MUM: 'Come on, Ruby, wake up. You'll be late for school.'

RUBY: 'I don't feel well Mum, I'll get up later.'

Aileen went downstairs wringing her hands. She told her husband, Maurice, that Ruby was unwell. They argued about who was going to stay at home and look after her. They both had important jobs, or so they thought. Maurice was the manager of the Yorkshire Building Society in York and Aileen was the manager of China China, a crockery outlet in the McArthur Glen Designer outlet.

MAURICE: 'I've got a meeting with the regional manager this morning at 9 o'clock; you'll have to stay and look after her.'

AILEEN: 'I can't. I've got a delivery coming this morning. I have to check it off against the list and sign for it. There's no one else can do it.'

It was stalemate. This always happened when there was anything wrong with Ruby. In the end, they did what they always did.

AILEEN: 'I'll ring mother.'

DORIS, AILEEN'S MOTHER: 'If you can't look after the child, you shouldn't have had her.'

Doris always said this. After she made her daughter squirm and grovel for what she thought was a suitable length of time, she agreed to come over and look after Ruby. She had done this quite a lot ever since Ruby was a baby, in fact. It's probably true to say that Doris had done more to bring Ruby up than her parents had. Ruby's parents gave her everything she asked for: computer, video recorder, TV, music centre, keyboard, two guitars, saxophone. They spent money on her, but they did not give her love and time. She got those from her grandmother.

Ruby Kind

Doris got on well with Ruby. It was clear to her early on that Ruby was a gifted child. She suggested to her daughter that she should send her to a private school that would nurture her talent but Aileen and Maurice never did anything about it. I don't think they gave much thought to Ruby. They were too caught up in their own lives.

Doris looked in at Ruby sound asleep in her bed. She left her alone. At lunchtime she came back and had another look. Ruby heard her and opened her eyes.

RUBY: 'Hallo, Gran.'

DORIS: 'Aah, back in the land of the living, are we? Good night, was it?'

Ruby grinned. She couldn't keep anything from her Gran.

RUBY: 'Great!'

DORIS: 'Tell me about it.'

Ruby described the loud music, the drum beat, the heaving mass of bodies, the lights, Yvonne, the bacon sandwiches.

RUBY: 'It was the best birthday I have ever had, Gran.'

DORIS: 'That's good dear. It does you good to let your hair down now and then.'

On Ruby's bedside cabinet, were two volumes of Winston Churchill's memoirs. Yvonne had fired Ruby's interest in history. She was reading about the second world war now. She had already read a book on Colditz and another on the Bouncing Bomb. Winston's was a bit heavy going, but it was interesting.

DORIS: 'I see you are reading about Winston. He was a great man, I met him, you know.'

RUBY: 'You actually met him? Where? When? Tell me about it, Gran.'

THE BLITZ

1940

LONDON

Four

Millions of tons of high explosive bombs fell on London in the Blitz between September 1940 and June 1941. They fell on other cities as well: Coventry, Birmingham, Bristol, Hull, but London was Hitler's main target. Some of the bombs were up to eight feet long. Some had deadly delayed fuses in them, as if the work of the Bomb Disposal teams wasn't dangerous enough with all the unexploded bombs about. They didn't know if the bomb they were working on had one of these delayed fuses in or not. It could explode at any minute. Many bomb disposal experts were killed or injured. COs: conscientious objectors often worked in bomb disposal.

All of Wren's churches in London were bombed during the war. Some were left little more than smouldering ruins. People look at these churches today and think they are looking at history, something that has been there for centuries. They are not. The churches were all rebuilt after the war. St Paul's Cathedral, Wren's masterpiece, was the exception. All around the Cathedral, the buildings were demolished by bombs, but no high explosive bomb landed on the Cathedral. Why was this? The German bombers used St Paul's Cathedral as a landmark on their way to bomb the docks. The Cathedral was exposed as it had never been before, and it did not escape entirely. Millions of incendiary bombs were also dropped by the Luftwaffe, as many as 100,000 in a single night. They exploded into flames on impact and caused untold damage. It was these incendiary bombs that fell on St Paul's. But early on in the conflict, the church had organised an army of volunteer fire watchers for St Paul's Cathedral and they patrolled the Cathedral every night. They knew where all the fire hydrants were, where the hosepipes were, the buckets of sand. When a fire bomb landed, they quickly put it out with water or sand. Sometimes they scooped it up in a shovel and threw it clear of the walls.

During all these air raids, the citizens of London sheltered wherever they could: in underground tube stations, in basements of large buildings, in church crypts. They also congregated in schools and other public buildings that offered no form of protection from the bombs whatsoever. People went there instead of staying in their homes. Some of these shelters suffered a direct hit from a bomb. Hundreds of people were killed in them including women and children. People were encouraged by the government to build Anderson shelters in their back garden, if they had a back garden. These were just a semi-circle of corrugated iron that you covered with earth. They were no use if they suffered a direct hit, but if your house was bombed, you usually survived if you were in your Anderson shelter.

At the beginning of the war, things were grim in the shelters. People just lay down on the cold, hard floor of the underground tube station and tried to get some sleep; they were at work in the morning. There was no sanitation, no food, nothing. After a few high profile visits by journalists and politicians, things started to improve. Bunk beds were brought in, so were chemical toilets, local hotels provided food, someone produced a squeeze box or a mouth organ. Some of the shelters took on an atmosphere of a party, they had a sing-song. The shelters were always crowded, people got there early to keep their place. Some lived down there.

At the beginning of the Blitz, children were evacuated to the country, but by Christmas 1940, many had come home to their parents in London, preferring to brave the bombs rather than be away from their parents in a stranger's house.

Christmas 1940 was notable for something else as well. On Christmas Eve, the German bombers didn't come. They didn't come on Christmas day either, or Boxing Day. People entertained the thought that maybe Hitler had given up on his bombing raids, but it was a false dawn. The day after, the bombers returned with a vengeance.

What the people of Britain didn't know was that on 9 January 1941, Hitler had inexplicably given orders to cease preparations for Operation Sealion: the invasion of Britain. He replaced it in June 1941 with Operation Barbarosa: the invasion of Russia. The bombing stopped.

Why did Hitler make this decision? What was the point of bombarding Britain for 10 months and not following through with an invasion? It is accepted in modern warfare that bombing is a precursor to invading a country. Would the Germans have succeeded in conquering Britain if they had invaded? The simple answer to that question is 'YES'. Churchill called it the biggest blunder in history.

It has happened before: Sir Francis Drake is credited with defeating the Spanish Armada. He didn't; it was the wind that defeated the Spanish Armada. Drake's attacks had little effect on the huge Spanish invasion force. But these were sailing ships and had no power; they went where the wind blew them, and it was strong that day, too strong to land. It blew them right down the English Channel and into the North Sea. The inexperienced Commander, the Duke of Medina, had had enough; he decided to head for home the hard way, around Scotland. He lost more ships on the rocky Scottish coast than Sir Francis Drake sank.

Neither of these events should have happened, but they did. Maybe someone was watching over them.

The Windmill Theatre was situated in the heart of Soho. Miraculously, it escaped the worst of the bombing, unlike the East End which took a pasting most nights. The nearest tube station to the Windmill was Tottenham Court Road. By the time Doris and the other girls got there in the early hours of the morning, it was packed. At first they ran from tube station to tube station, basement to basement, desperately trying to find shelter from the bombs. But after a while, they didn't bother and just bedded down in the ticket hall of Tottenham Court Road, which offered them no protection from the falling bombs whatsoever. One night, the ticket hall suffered a direct hit: a thousand pounder crashed through the roof and exploded. Everyone there was killed. Fortunately, Doris was working that night.

The Windmill was putting on a special show for Winston Churchill, the Prime Minister, and his cabinet. They had the place to themselves. The curtain rose to reveal 5 girls in fancy bikinis and headdresses.

The girls left and Arthur Askey walked onto the stage.

ARTHUR: 'Hallo, playmates! A funny thing happened to me on my way here. Excuse me laughing; I know what's coming.'

The curtain rose to reveal a row of naked girls, including Doris. They went off and Max Miller came on the stage.

MAX: 'You may wonder why I'm dressed like this. I'm dressed like this because I've been to a wedding. I'm a bit tired. I've been shoplifting and some of those shops are very heavy, I can tell you.'

At the end of the show, all the girls and the comedians lined up on the stage and Churchill walked along talking to them and shaking their hands. He had a twinkle in his eye when he told them that they were helping the war effort.

RUBY: 'Didn't you mind, standing there naked in front of all those men?'

DORIS: 'Oh no, you got used to it. It was just a job. We were comfortable, you see. They always kept the place warm. The men were hot under the collar, but we were fine. It wouldn't have been right if the girls had goose bumps.'

RUBY: 'Did any of the comedians try it on?'

DORIS: 'The new ones did for a while. The old ones didn't bother. In fact they said it ruined their sex life. They weren't excited by the sight of a naked woman anymore. Except for Sid James; he was a devil.'

Five

Doris lived in sheltered housing: a flat overlooking Rowntree Park. It was warm, comfortable, there was always someone around to talk to. Regular outings were organised for you if you wanted them and the press of a button would bring a warden rushing to you if you needed help. It suited her fine, but she still missed Vincent, she always would.

They had met in the Military Hospital in York, during the war. Doris was a nurse and Vincent was a patient. After a couple of years, Doris got bored with stripping and retrained as a nurse at Guy's Hospital in London. She received a letter from her mother telling her that Tom, her brother, had been wounded and was in the Military Hospital in York, recovering. Doris applied for a fortnight's leave and caught a train to York.

Tom was worse than she had been led to believe by her mother. His right leg had been blown off just above the knee. They had operated at the field hospital at Monte Cassino, but they had left him too long; gangrene had set in. They flew Tom back to England and onto the Military Hospital in his home town of York. The surgeons operated on his leg again, trying to stop the advance of the gangrene, but it was too late. There was nothing they could do. It was just a matter of time.

The Hospital was short staffed, too many patients, not enough nurses, and doctors. So Doris put on her nurse's uniform and nursed her brother herself. She also nursed Vincent and several other of the men.

Vincent was an Italian prisoner of war. He too had been wounded at the battle of Monte Cassino. He had been shot in the lung and had difficulty breathing. He was in the next bed to Tom. They hadn't got the time or the space to segregate prisoners from British servicemen; they were all mixed in together and treated the same. This was common on both sides of the conflict. Vincent couldn't speak English, but he was a mime artist. Mime theatres were popular in Italy before the war; you can still find them today if you know where to look. Vincent made them all laugh puling funny faces, making extravagant gestures and strange noises, until he was convulsed in a fit of coughing. Doris told him to be careful, but she laughed along with everyone else.

At the end of her fortnight's leave, the Sister asked Doris to step inside her office.

SISTER: 'You seem to have made yourself indispensable, Doris. Quite frankly, I don't know what we would have done without you this last fortnight. I think we had better offer you a job.'

DORIS: 'Thankyou, Sister. I was worried about leaving Tom.'

SISTER: 'That's settled then. I'll ring Guy's. Don't worry, they'll understand.'

Inevitably, Tom died. Vincent insisted on going to his funeral. He shouldn't have been out of bed, really. The only clothes he had were his Italian Army uniform, which wouldn't have been appropriate at a British soldier's funeral. So they had a search round and found him an old brown suit. It didn't fit of course. Throughout the service, Vincent held Doris's hand.

Doris is a modest woman. If you had asked her about it, she would have just said that she did her job, but she saved Vincent's life, no doubt about that.

Doris and Vincent got married as soon as Vincent was well enough to leave the Hospital. Vincent was sent to work on a farm along with other Italian prisoners of war. But he wasn't allowed to live with Doris until after the war had finished. Doris was six months' pregnant with Jonah before they finally managed to persuade the Landlord to let them rent the farm. There was a lot of animosity towards Italians at the time. But the sight of Doris's bulging belly and Vincent's amusing personality, particularly his mimes, won the landlord over and he agreed to let them rent the farm.

Vincent had been dead for ten years now. They were married for 46 years and had bought the farm from the landlord. In his will, Vincent left the farm to their son Jonah. To his daughter, Aileen, he left a row of four old farmworker's cottages. They had been empty for a while and they didn't have running water and electricity but they were structurally sound and the roof didn't leak. Gradually, Aileen and Maurice were refurbishing the cottages and letting them out as holiday lets. They had done three, there was one more to go. It was debatable which of Doris's two children had got the better deal. Aileen had tenants for most of the summer from May to October but Jonah struggled to make money out of the farm.

Doris stayed on at the farm after Jonah and Dinah moved in. Dinah was Jonah's wife. They had been married 20 years but they still behaved like love-struck teenagers. They had been unable to have children; Dinah had endometriosis. Instead of driving them apart, as often happened, Jonah and Dinah became even closer. Doris said she felt like a gooseberry. When she got the chance of the flat, she jumped at it.

Five years ago, Dinah had died of breast cancer. Jonah was devastated. He felt like his soul had been ripped from him. He couldn't believe that she would never walk back through the door. Sometimes, when he was sat watching television, Jonah turned his head quickly to look at the door, expecting Dinah to walk through it, but, of course, she never did.

The doctor gave Jonah anti-depressants, but he couldn't get on with them. They made him feel funny. He started going down the pub. Jonah and Dinah hadn't drunk much, just the occasional bottle of wine. Now Jonah drank 5 or 6 pints a night. He had discovered that when he drank, he lost his memory. He couldn't remember walking home, getting into bed. His drinking mates started telling him things he had done down the pub: he was stood at the bar, a full pint of beer in his hand and the pint slipped from his grasp and smashed on the floor. The landlord had been annoyed, bustling round, sweeping up the glass and mopping the beer. Jonah didn't remember anything about it when he walked into the bar the following night and the landlord made a comment about it. He was unsteady on his feet when he had been drinking: they were all piling out the pub at closing time with Jonah at the front when, without warning, he collapsed on the floor in the doorway and everyone fell on top of him. They thought it a laugh, but, again, Jonah didn't remember. There was one thing they told him he had done that Jonah couldn't dispute: he had fallen down a hole that BT had dug in the pavement, smashed through the barriers, and landed face first in the mud. When he woke up the next morning, his clothes were covered in mud and when he looked in the mirror, so were his face and hands.

Jonah would have stopped all this drinking if it wasn't for one thing: whilst he was drunk, he didn't think about Dinah; he couldn't feel the great gaping hole inside where she had once been. Jonah drank to forget. It was the only thing he had found that worked.

When Jonah and Dinah took over the farm, it had a dairy herd. It was Jonah's father's pride and joy, but it proved to be too much like hard work for Jonah and he sold the cows. The farm was mainly arable now: wheat, oilseed rape, sugar beet, apart from a few sheep. There were about 60 sheep in the top paddock. He didn't make much money out of them; he kept them for just one reason: he loved lambing time. He always had, right from when he was a boy helping his father on the farm. He loved all that new life, the exuberant lambs jumping for joy.

It was coming up for the second week in February and the first lambs had arrived. Jonah had brought the sheep down and put them in pens in his big barn. He had stopped drinking. He didn't need to drink, he was happy. He was a nice man again, like he had been before he lost Dinah.

Ruby loved lambing too. She spent as much time at the farm as she could, after school and at weekends. She even stayed the night some weekends, sitting up with her Uncle Jonah, helping the sheep give birth. Mostly they did it on their own, but now and then you had to lend a hand. At first Jonah called the vet to help quite a lot with difficult births, but the vet was a busy man and had shown Jonah what to do. Jonah only called him now if he was really stuck.

It was one in the morning. Jonah and Ruby were sat on a bale of straw having just helped a ewe with twins. The mother was licking the little lambs. They were trying to stand up, their tails going like mad.

Ruby took the top off a flask she had made and poured them both some tea.

RUBY: 'I'm thinking of forming a group, Uncle Jonah. It's early days yet. I haven't told anyone else about it. If I do, can we use the barn for practice?'

JONAH: 'Yeah, of course. It's empty most of the year. I only use it for lambing. What sort of group are you thinking of forming?'

RUBY: 'That's the trouble. I don't know. My record collection is so varied, I would need everything from a Rock band to a full orchestra. I need to drill down into a particular style and put a collection of songs together, but I don't know where to start.'

JONAH: 'I may be able to help you there.'

Jonah walked over to the other side of the barn, pulled out two bales of straw, and walked through the gap. Ruby followed him. He switched on a light and against the wall was row upon row of vinyl records.

RUBY: 'Wow! Where did you get this lot, Uncle Jonah?'

JONAH: 'It's a long story. We had sold the dairy cows and planted up the fields and there really wasn't much to do. Dinah was reading the Press. She turned to the back page and read out an advert.'

DINAH: *'House clearance – All areas. We buy antiques and vintage.'*

'We could do that; we've got the barn and the horse box. It would be fun. I love looking around other people's houses. You never know, we might find a valuable antique and make our fortunes.'

JONAH: 'We don't know anything about antiques.'

DINAH: 'We'll pick it up. Oh say we can, Jonah. It's so exciting.'

Jonah laughed at Dinah's enthusiasm. Her face was a picture.

JONAH: 'Alright. I'll go down to the Press tomorrow and put an advert in.'

Nothing happened for a couple of weeks, then they got three enquiries in as many days. They were in business. The first was an old lady's bungalow. She had dementia and had been in a home for about six months. She had fought them when they said she had to sell her bungalow to pay for her care, but she was getting worse. Some days she had to try really hard to remember who her son was. Her son was called Frank and he was her only child. She told Frank to put the bungalow up for sale.

Frank met Jonah and Dinah at the bungalow. He walked round with them, room by room.

FRANK: 'What do you think?'

DINAH: 'Well, there's nothing of any real value, Mr Franklin. We will probably have to take quite a bit of it to the tip, which, as I am sure you are aware, the Council charge us for. Apart from one thing.'

Dinah walked over to the mantlepiece and picked up a small, brass carriage clock.

DINAH: 'This is nice. I tell you what I'll do. If you let me have this, I'll give you a hundred pound in cash and we'll have the place cleared for you within 24 hours.'

Frank beamed. Dinah had just taken a weight off his shoulders. He had a cash buyer for the bungalow but they wanted it cleared.

FRANK: 'You've got yourself a deal.'

They all shook hands. Frank gave them a key and Dinah counted out a hundred pounds. Jonah waited till Frank had gone out of the door.

JONAH: 'Where did that come from?'

Dinah laughed.

DINAH: 'I don't know. I just sort of made it up as I went along.'

JONAH: 'And the clock? You made that up as well?'

DINAH: 'I already had a look at the back. It has a proper movement, not a battery, so I guessed it could be valuable.'

JONAH: 'There are hidden depths to you Dinah Magrioni, that I know nothing about.'

DINAH: 'A girl has to have a few secrets.'

Dinah took photographs of some of the stuff and put it on Ebay. She underestimated the cost of postage and packing at first and made a small loss, but she had got the hang of it now and was enjoying herself. She took the carriage clock to an antique dealer in Stonegate. The old gentleman screwed his eyeglass in his eye and examined it carefully. He took his time. His name was Mr Middleditch.

MR MIDDLEDITCH: 'You are very fortunate to have brought this clock to me, Mrs Magrioni. It is a very fine clock, a Drocourt Repeating Bell striking carriage clock, an early one, by the looks of it. Can I ask why you have chosen my establishment?'

DINAH: 'Oh, I've passed by this shop for years. I always look in the window. I bought my mother a bracelet from here for her silver wedding anniversary. You probably don't remember me.'

MR MIDDLEDITCH: 'Now you mention it, your face does look familiar. I never forget a face. To return to your clock, may I ask how you happened to come by it?'

Dinah told him about her and Jonah's new business. Mr Middleditch thought for a few moments.

MR MIDDLEDITCH: 'May I propose an informal arrangement between ourselves? You bring me anything you think may be of value and I will give you a fair and reasonable price. I am afraid there are unscrupulous dealers in this business, Mrs Magrioni. If you had gone somewhere else, you might not have realised the full value of this clock. It is worth two thousand pounds. Dinah's legs turned to jelly. Mr Middleditch moved surprisingly quickly and pulled out a chair for her.

Dinah and Jonah did a few more house clearances. They were at one now: a large 3 storey Victorian terraced house in Bishopthorpe Road. The old lady who lived there had recently lost her husband and was moving in with her daughter who lived in Oxford. She had a small hotel and Mrs Oxley was going to live in the annex. They weren't going to sell the house. They were going to convert it into three flats and let them to students. They would buy new furniture for each flat so Mrs Oxley's furniture wasn't needed. Dinah and Jonah walked round the house with Mrs Oxley. Dinah had a notebook and jotted things down in it. They had finished the first two floors.

DINAH: 'I'd like an antique dealer to look at your furniture, Mrs Oxley. I think some of it could be quite valuable. I'm not an expert, but I know someone who is. He will give us the true value of what it's worth.'

MRS OXLEY: 'Thankyou dear. I didn't expect that. You could have taken it all and not said a word.'

JONAH: 'We're not like that, Mrs Oxley.'

MRS OXLEY: 'Perhaps I can repay the favour. Have a look on the top floor. There may be something there that surprises you. I can't get up there myself these days.'

Jonah opened a door. Inside, the room was filled with row upon row of vinyl records. Every wall was lined with them. In the corner was a very expensive looking Hi-Fi and a large leather swivel chair.

Jonah came back downstairs, slightly out of breath.

JONAH: 'That's amazing, Mrs Oxley. I haven't got a clue what they are worth.'

MRS OXLEY: 'Take them. Those records have caused enough hard feeling in this house. My husband used to spend more time with them than he did with me.'

JONAH: 'Well, if you're sure.'

MRS OXLEY: 'Sure I'm sure. I have never been so sure of anything in my life.'

Dinah was doing well selling on Ebay, but still things were piling up and Jonah was worried. Dinah wasn't worried. She simply rang Mr Middleditch and he arranged for an auction right there in the barn. They sold everything except an old upright piano and a settee that they really should have taken to the tip, oh, and the records, of course. Jonah had hidden them behind a great pile of straw bales. He was wading his way through them. Not just Jonah: Dinah liked them too. Especially the rock n roll records. They used to jive in the barn like teenagers.

Six

Jonah looked sad when he finished telling the tale.

RUBY: 'Are you alright, Uncle Jonah?'

JONAH: 'Mmm, I don't know if I will ever be alright again, Ruby.'

A lamb had escaped from its pen and was running around the barn. Jonah ran after it and scooped it up. The lamb bleated. Jonah tickled it under its chin and put it back with its mother. He walked back to the records.

JONAH: 'They are in alphabetical order: A top right, to Z bottom left. The ones I have listened to have been from the fifties, sixties, and seventies, but I have only listened to about a third. If you can't get enough songs out of this lot for your group, I'll eat my cap.'

Ruby laughed, reached up and pulled out the first record. It was by Amen Corner.

JONAH: 'The single is called 'Wide eyed and Legless'. I remember it. Very appropriate for me, I suppose.'

Ruby Kind

RUBY: 'What on earth is filed under Z? I've never heard of a group beginning with Z.'

JONAH: 'Ah, that's a good one. The group has an unusual name, which is something in itself. But the track to look out for is the last one. It's called Whopper. Have a look at the sleeve note.'

Ruby was missing school, but in actual fact, she was working very hard. She spent every hour she could in Jonah's barn, listening to the records, selecting the ones she liked and writing down the lyrics. She had moved her keyboard and computer into the barn and was writing the music as well. Ruby could write music like other people write letters. She didn't just write the main tune, she wrote arrangements for each instrument, apart from the drums. She didn't know how to write music for the drums. Miss Eyeball, the music teacher didn't think it was necessary. When Ruby asked her how to write drum music, she wanted to know why. Ruby told her she was thinking of forming a group.

MISS EYEBALL: 'Is that why you have been missing school, Ruby?'

Ruby nodded.

MISS EYEBALL: 'Tell me about it.'

Ruby told her teacher what she had been doing.

MISS EYEBALL: 'I admire your ambition, Ruby, but you must attend school. It's important. You'll get into trouble otherwise.'

RUBY: 'OK, Miss.'

MISS EYEBALL: 'If I find out for you how to write drum music, will you promise me you'll come to school?'

RUBY: 'Yes, Miss. Thanks Miss.'

Unfortunately, the damage had been done. A letter arrived for Ruby's parents from the headmaster telling them of Ruby's absences from school. He requested their presence in his office at 10 o'clock on Wednesday morning. Ruby's father shouted at her at the breakfast table.

MAURICE: 'What's going on, Ruby?' Why aren't you going to school?'

RUBY: 'School's boring.'

MAURICE: 'I don't care if it's boring or not, young lady. You must go. You've got to get some qualifications to go to university. It's the only way you are going to get a decent job. Look at your mother and me. We've both got decent jobs. You don't want to end up on the tills in Tesco, do you?'

RUBY: 'I quite like Tesco.'

AILEEN: 'Don't be facetious, Ruby. You know what your father means. Is there something else? Are you being bullied?'

RUBY: 'Just let them try! They'll get back more than they bargained for.'

MAURICE: 'God knows how I am going to make this meeting. I am up to my eyes in it.'

AILEEN: 'Me too.'

MAURICE: 'This is just too bad, Ruby. I won't stand anymore of it. If you don't go to school, I am taking all your things off you.'

He meant all the electrical equipment and musical instruments that Ruby had in her bedroom.

MAURICE: 'Oh God, look at the time. I'm going to be late. I'll have to go. I haven't finished with you, Ruby. I mean to get to the bottom of this.'

Aileen took Ruby to school in her car. Neither of them spoke a word.

At lunchtime, Ruby went round to see her Uncle Jonah. He was in the top paddock, watching the lambs. They had all been born now and were happily gambolling about in the field.

RUBY: 'Uncle Jonah, can I move into the farmhouse with you? It'll save all this toing and froing from home that I have to do setting up the band.'

It's true Ruby had been spending all her evenings and weekends at the farm, plus quite a few days when she should have been at school.

RUBY: 'I'll take that as a 'yes' then.'

JONAH: 'Please yourself, Ruby. You know what I'm like.'

Ruby hired a taxi and moved all her stuff into the farm. She left a note on her bed. It said:

'To save you any more bother, I have moved out.
If you are interested, I'll be at Uncle Jonah's.

Ruby'

Aileen found the note. She showed it to Maurice. Maurice rang Jonah. No one answered the phone.

Ruby and Jonah were in the barn, tidying away the pens for another year when Ruby's parents rolled up in the Audi. They watched them knock at the farmhouse door.

JONAH: 'You had better go and see them, Ruby. Something tells me this move of yours isn't as straightforward as it seems.'

Ruby walked up silently and stood behind her parents. They turned and jumped.

AILEEN: 'Ruby! What the devil do you think you are doing? You frightened the life out of us. Get your things. We are taking you back home.'

RUBY: 'No, Mum. I'm staying here. You can't make me. I'm over 16.'

MAURICE: 'I don't care whether you are over 16 or not. You are not staying here with that drunkard.'

Unseen by any of them Jonah had moved up behind them.

JONAH: 'Drunkard, is it, Maurice? Mum says you are not fit to have a child. You can't look after her. If Ruby needs looking after, you call her! It seems to me she will be better off here. We get on well. We work together. Yes, I drink a bit. There's a reason for that. Maybe Ruby can help me. I don't know. What I do know is that I enjoy her company. Something that you seem to be indifferent to.'

Jonah had hit a nerve with Maurice and Aileen. They both knew that what he said was true.

MAURICE: 'I'll give you a couple of weeks, Ruby. You'll soon come running back once you see what Jonah is really like.'

Maurice and Aileen got back into the Audi and sped off, the wheels spinning on the gravel surface.

RUBY: 'Thanks, Uncle Jonah.'

JONAH: 'I enjoyed that.'

Funnily enough, Ruby went to school every day after that. Well, she had promised Miss Eyeball, but she wasn't listening to the class most of the time, she was writing arrangements in her head.

Miss Eyeball rang round her music friends and they came up with a name: Nathan Watterly. He was retired now, in his seventies. He lived in a large, terraced house off Bootham. They all said he was very good. Miss Eyeball gave him a ring. Nathan said he would be happy to give Ruby some lessons. He wasn't bothered about getting paid. He just said: 'Send the girl round. She sounds promising.'

Ruby knocked on the big black door with the big, brass knocker. A tall man with a shock of white hair answered.

NATHAN: 'Ah, you must be Ruby.'

RUBY: 'Yes. And you must be Nathan Watterly.'

NATHAN: 'The very same. Come inside flower.'

Ruby walked into the tiled hall and followed Nathan into the lounge. It was comfortably furnished with a red velvet three piece suite, black velvet curtains and a cream carpet.

NATHAN: 'Sit yourself down and I'll put the kettle on. We'll have a chat.'

Nathan returned with two willow patterned mugs and a plate of chocolate biscuits.

NATHAN: 'Before we get down to business, Ruby, I think we should get acquainted. Tell me about this group you are forming.'

RUBY: 'Well, I haven't actually formed it yet. I have been busy writing the music.'

NATHAN: 'Composing?'

RUBY: 'No. My Uncle Jonah has a large collection of vinyl records. I've been listening to them and selecting tracks that I like. Some of them are very good. I've been writing arrangements for each of the instruments: keyboard, bass, lead guitar, rhythm guitar. Now I want to write an arrangement for the drums. I know it's not usual; most groups let the musicians do their own arrangements, but I don't seem able to do that. I like to write it myself. I suppose I like to be in control. I'm a control freak, is that bad?'

NATHAN: 'No, as a matter of fact, it's very good. Very professional actually. It's what Andrew Lloyd Webber does.'

RUBY: 'Really? I never knew that.'

NATHAN: 'I can certainly help you with the drums. I've had a lot of experience. Let me give you a potted history.

I started in the sixties with The Bloggs. We had a couple of hits: 'Wild Thing' and 'I Can't Control Myself'. After that, I had a spell with The Earth Band. You won't know these bands, love. They are before your time.'

Ruby had listened to The Bloggs and The Earth Band but she didn't interrupt. Nathan was in full spate.

NATHAN: After The Earth Band split up, I was out of work for a while. I managed to get a few sessions at various recording studios in London, but it was hard to manage stuff. I had finished a session at Abbey Road and decided to go down the pub for a drink, the Lily Langtry. I bumped into Helen Row. I knew Helen from way back. We got talking and she told me she had switched from pop to jazz. She was doing so well that she had decided to form her own band. When I told her I was looking for work, she offered me the job of drummer. I had to learn jazz quick. Helen put me in touch with Ken Bat's drummer and the rest, as they say, is history. I've been with Helen ever since. We haven't split up; we just haven't played for a while. I guess we are all getting old. Have you finished your tea?'

RUBY: 'Yes, thank you.'

NATHAN: 'Come on then, let's go bash some skins.'

Ruby was a quick learner. Nathan gave her his old drum kit. He had meant to sell it, but had never got round to it. It was just gathering dust in the corner of the basement. Nathan's music room was in the basement.

Seven

Ruby had no trouble recruiting for her group. All her class knew she was a brilliant musician, they all wanted to be in it. The problem, as she knew it would be, was the drums.

RUBY: 'I've learned to play the drums so if any one fancies it, I can teach you.'

Jason Routledge said he would give it a bash. Jason played the xylophone. He was a big lad, over six foot, a rugby player, very fit. Ruby thought his build would be an advantage. She always felt completely knackered after she had had a session on the drums with Nathan.

RUBY: 'OK. Come round to the farm. I've got a drum kit. We can make as much noise as we like there. You can have a try out, see what you think. For everyone else who is interested. I suggest we meet every lunchtime in the hall until we sort out the final line-up.'

Ruby had a good idea who she wanted. She just wanted to put them through their paces.

A couple of weeks later, the group met for the first time in Jonah's barn on Saturday morning. They were sat on straw bales in front of Jonah's vinyl record collection. Ruby explained a bit about the records and how she had selected tracks for them to play. She handed them each their music.

Ruby's Band

Kirsty Wheatfield – Bass and vocals

Evan Smith – Lead guitar

Ade Montgolfier – Rhythm guitar and vocals

Jason Routledge – Drums

Ruby Fish – Keyboards and vocals

EVAN: 'Jeez, Ruby, you wrote all this!'

Ruby laughed.

RUBY: 'Now you know why I missed a few lessons. How long do you think it will take to learn?'

EVAN: 'Learning could take a while, but there is no reason why we shouldn't have a run through. We've got the music. It'd be just like playing a new piece for the orchestra.'

JASON: 'It may take me a while longer.'

RUBY: 'Don't worry, Jason. We all know you are starting from scratch. You've got the hardest job of all of us. There's no need to put ourselves under pressure. It's not like we have a gig coming up or anything. Why don't we meet back here in two weeks' time and see how it goes?'

They all agreed to that.

RUBY: 'Before you go, I'd like to play you something. The records are in alphabetical order. I was curious what was filed under Z. My Uncle Jonah pulled out this record – and there's a track on it called Whopper. Before I play it to you, I'll just read the sleeve note.'

> *'I was having difficulty going to the toilet. I hadn't opened my bowels for about 6 weeks and I was getting worried. I went to the doctor and he tried me on every type of laxative that he could think of but nothing worked. He decided to send me for a Barium Meal, which isn't a meal at all. Before I went for the Barium Meal, I had to take a very strong laxative that they sent me from the hospital the night before. I took the first sachet and nothing happened, then I took the second. Within 10 minutes, I had to rush to the toilet, going like a machine gun.*
>
> *At the hospital, I lay on a metal table and a nurse shoved this tube up my arse and poured in some liquid. The table rolled from side to side and up and down. A bloke sat behind a screen and looked at my bowels on a computer. When it had finished, he came rushing out and*

told me: 'good news, you haven't got cancer.' I was a bit shocked. No one had mentioned cancer before. He couldn't say exactly what the problem was, but I had a loop in my bowel that had probably caused a blockage. He told me to get more fibre in my diet and take a laxative every morning.

I did what he said and was overjoyed when I produce a big, brown turd the next morning. Ever since then, I have kept a close eye on what comes out of my rear end, punching the air and saying 'YES!' every time I do a big brown turd. I had been doing this for a couple of weeks, when the first line of a song came into my head. It wasn't much of a line, only four words. Over the weeks and months, those four words developed into a full blown song called 'Whopper!'

Drum break Introduction

Male vocals

I done a whopper, done a whopper, done a whopper
I done a whopper, a whopper I have done

I done a whopper, done a whopper, done a whopper
I done a whopper, a whopper I have done

Trumpet and guitar solo
Female vocals – verse
Drum solo
Junior School Choir vocals – verse
Junior School recorder solo
Football crowd vocals – verse
Trumpet and Xylophone solo
End with drum break

By the time the track finished, they were all singing along, laughing.

JASON: 'Cracking song. We must do it. There's even a xylophone in it. How good is that!'

KIRSTY: 'Where on earth did they get the name from?

RUBY: 'It's from an old song.'

Now she had got the group off the ground, Ruby's attention turned to finding a name for it. She couldn't just call it 'Ruby's Band'; that would be a cop out. She started carrying a little book in her pocket and jotted down names as she thought of them:

Ruby Kind

Triffic
Graffiti
Ergo
The crunch
Frog spawn

She was strangely drawn to Frog spawn. When she was a little girl, she had caught some frog spawn from the pond in the top paddock in her Grandma's farm. She put it in the bucket under the sink and forgot about it. The frogs hatched out. There were loads of little frogs jumping all over the kitchen. Her mother had screamed. She didn't like 'jumpy things'. She wasn't a farmer's daughter at all.

This was no good. She mustn't be silly. She couldn't possibly call the group Frog Spawn. She must be sensible. She had put a lot of work into this group. She was sat in the big leather swivel chair in front of the records in the barn one evening looking at her list. She had added to it:

White water
Unbelievable
Frankincense
Purple People Eaters

Absentmindedly, she reached out, pulled down a record and put it on. She didn't look at what she had selected. As she listened, a smile spread over her face.

Ruby didn't think she was anything like the girl in the song, but she liked the name. Maybe she could have a stage name, plenty of people had stage names: Elton John, Ringo Starr, Engelbert Humperdink. Ruby had laughed when she found this last name amongst her Uncle's records. She thought it was the wrong way round. Surely if your name really was Engelbert Humperdink you would change it at the first opportunity, to change your name TO Engelbert Humperdink was perverse.

She decided to call the group Ruby Kind. She may even call herself Ruby Kind. She hadn't decided yet. She was quite proud of her surname Fish. The Fish family had a claim to fame: Michael Fish, the weatherman; Michael was Ruby's father's cousin.

Michael infamously announced to the nation that the hurricane heading for the south coast would pass harmlessly by out to sea. It didn't. It struck the south coast with a ferocity that had never been seen before in England. It laid waste to a huge swathe of countryside from the south coast right into London including Tresco Abbey gardens in the Isles of Scilly and Kew Gardens in London. In 1987, the hurricane uprooted trees, blew off roofs and tossed cars about like toys. The Fish family gathered protectively around Michael, but it was no use. The press wanted a scapegoat and they hung Michael out to dry. It wasn't even his fault. All he did was read out the computer forecast as he always did. It could have been any of the weathermen: Bill Giles, John Ketley, Ian McCaskill, they could have all given the same forecast. Unfortunately, for Michael Fish, he drew the short straw. It was an ignominious end to a very fine weatherman's career.

Eight

Vincent and Doris rented the farm for a couple of years, then they got the opportunity to buy it. The landlord was emigrating to America. The first thing Vincent and Doris knew about it was when an agent came round the farm to value it. The landlord had never considered that Vincent and Doris would have the wherewithal to buy the farm.

Vincent disappeared to Italy for a week. When he came back, he offered the landlord cash for the farm. The landlord was suspicious at first; he wanted to know where Vincent had got hold of such a large amount of money. Vincent gave him two letters: one from his family in Italy and one from his family's bank manager in Italy. Both letters were in Italian, which the landlord didn't read so an interpreter had to be found. This took time. In the meantime, other people were expressing interest in the farm and having a look around. Vincent and Doris tried to put them off, saying what a bad harvest they had had last year and how the bottom field was prone to flooding.

Having got the letters translated, the landlord was impressed by Vincent's family and, for the first time, talked to him like an equal. He accepted Vincent's cash offer for the farm with gratitude and wished him well for the future.

Doris would have liked to have read the translations of those two letters, but the landlord kept them, together with the original. These days, it is an easy thing to make a photocopy of a document that you want to keep, but in those days there were no such things as photocopiers. Copies had to be made by hand. Doris didn't get the opportunity to do that.

At the time, Vincent couldn't speak much English. When Doris asked him how he had come by the money to buy the farm, all he could say was 'it is my inheritance.'

Ruby had always wondered about her grandfather's Italian family. She wished she had asked him about it whilst he was still alive. But she had been too young. Vincent died when she was only six. She could remember him as a nice, kind man who made her laugh, but that was about all she could remember.

In the year 2000, the internet was just starting to come into its own. Computers were a 'foreign country' to Jonah, but Ruby used her computer every day. She found it invaluable for writing music.

Websites were starting to appear on the internet that enabled you to trace your family tree. Ruby clicked onto one and typed: 'Vincent Magrioni'. She showed Jonah what she had found. He was fascinated. She was using a site called 'Ancestry'. She typed in Vincent Magrioni and followed the links.

Jonah sat with Ruby whilst she researched the Magrioni family tree. He was amazed at what she found out. The hours flew by. He didn't feel the need to go down the pub so often. His mind was occupied by Ruby's research. He sometimes went two or three hours without thinking about Dinah.

Ruby was pleased by the improvement in Jonah. She started thinking about his future. He needed a lady friend. There was a dance at the Assembly Rooms, old time ballroom. She knew if she asked Jonah if he wanted to go he would say no, so she just told him she was taking him somewhere special and he must smarten himself up, wear his best suit.

There was a good crowd at the dance. People of all ages, not just older people you would expect. Jonah kept glancing towards the door. He wasn't pleased with Ruby. She had tricked him. Nevertheless, he let her lead him onto the dance floor for a waltz. A group of four middle aged women were sat on the next table. Ruby got talking to them. Jonah just sat and drank his beer. The next dance was the foxtrot. Ruby didn't know how to do the foxtrot. She asked if one of the women would dance with her uncle. Rhonda had listened to Ruby's potted history of her uncle and wondered if he was worth a chance. She was on her own now her daughter had gone away to university. She never thought she would look at another man after Colin, but she found herself saying yes, she would love to dance. Ruby stood up and took hold of Jonah's hand.

RUBY: 'Next dance, Uncle Jonah.'

Jonah got to his feet and Ruby introduced him to Rhonda. She then left them and went off to the bar. Jonah and Rhonda looked at each other for a few moments. Then they both laughed.

JONAH: 'She's a fine girl. I think she's trying to fix us up.'

RHONDA: 'It seems a shame to disappoint her. Shall we dance?'

JONAH: 'Why not. I'm afraid I may be a bit rusty.'

RHONDA: 'Me too, not to worry. We'll work it out together.'

Jonah and Rhonda stayed on the dance floor for the next dance. It was another waltz only this time there was a singer.

Come Dance with me

Male vocals

> *I can hardly wait, makes my poor heart ache*
> *I won't hesitate, though it's getting late*
> *Because I love you, better than I did before*
>
> *Come dance with me, I want to be*
> *Held closely in your arms like yesterday*
> *The stage is set, I've no regrets*
> *So listen as the band begins to play*

Female vocals

Repeat above

Ruby danced with an old gentleman who looked to be about 90. He was a very good dancer though; he led her round, patiently teaching her the steps.

By the end of the evening, Jonah and Rhonda were sat closely together, talking. Jonah hadn't even finished his first pint. Unfortunately, Rhonda was off on a cruise to the Norwegian fjords with her sister next week so she couldn't see Jonah, but they agreed to meet in Betty's in a fortnight's time.

Ruby Kind

Jonah was on his own in the farmhouse. Ruby had gone out somewhere. He missed her, ridiculous. A young girl like Ruby couldn't babysit a full grown man like him all the time.

JONAH: 'Get a grip, Jonah, sort yourself out.'

He decided to go down the pub. He hadn't been for a while. He would just have a couple, no need to stay late. His drinking mates greeted him like a long lost friend. There were four of them. They each bought a round. Before he knew what he was doing, Jonah was halfway down his fourth pint.

As usual, he didn't remember walking home. When he woke up the next morning, he found that he had got his pyjama bottoms on back to front, he still had one sock on and his clothes were left in a heap in the middle of the bedroom. At least he had got undressed. Sometimes he woke up fully dressed, laid on top of the bed.

When he got downstairs, Ruby had already left for school. She had left out eggs and bacon for his breakfast, but Jonah didn't fancy friend food. His stomach was a bit queasy. He put the eggs and bacon back in the fridge and poured himself a bowl of cornflakes.

He ate slowly. Something had happened last night in the pub; he was sure of it. But he couldn't for the life of him remember what it was. He finished his breakfast and put the bowl in the sink. He didn't bother washing it up.

Jonah climbed into his Land Rover and set off to check on how his crops were growing. It had been a hot dry summer this year. They were not as advanced as he would have liked them to be. He was worried. What he needed was a good heavy downpour. Jonah looked up into a clear blue sky. No chance. He was halfway to his first oil seed rape field when he realised he hadn't had a cup of tea this morning. There was no one there to remind him. Left to his own devices, he forgot all sorts of things these days.

Ruby was taking her GCSEs n a couple of months' time. She was busy in the dining room putting together her Art portfolio. She had all her paintings and drawings spread out on the large dining room table. Jonah picked one up. It was a painting of a swan on Rowntree Park Lake. It was beautiful.

JONAH: 'This is good, Ruby.'

RUBY: 'Thanks. I've got to decide which ones to put forward for my GCSE. I just can't make up my mind.'

JONAH: 'I shouldn't worry, Ruby. They're all good. I didn't realise you were such a talented girl.'

Ruby blushed.

RUBY: 'That's the nicest thing you have ever said to me, Uncle Jonah.'

JONAH: 'I've got a bit of business to do. I shouldn't be late. If it will help, I'll have a look at your pictures with you when I get back.'

RUBY: 'Thanks, Uncle Jonah. I'll still be here!'

Jonah's business was down the pub. He wanted to find out what had gone on last night. It was a good job he did. Jonah's drinking mates were waiting for him when he walked into the pub. They greeted him with cries of 'Come and have a drink, partner.'

Jonah didn't know what they were talking about. He refused any alcoholic drink and ordered a pint of coca cola. They were all shocked.

JONAH: 'Right then, in your own time. Tell me exactly what happened last night.'

TED: 'A trainer came into the pub. He bought us all a drink. He said he had had two winners and felt like celebrating. The trainer told us about his two winners. One of the horses that won he had to sell. It was a grey, a beautiful horse. Its owner was emigrating to Australia and didn't want to take her with him.

TRAINER: 'I don't suppose you chaps would be interested would you? He wants £5,000 for her, but seeing as there are four of you, I could let you have her for a thousand pounds each. You could own a leg each.'

Jonah was the only one of the group that had been to a horse race meeting. He used to go with his father to York races, but that was over 20 years ago. Apparently he had persuaded the others to shake hands on the deal. No money had been exchanged yet, they would view the horse on Sunday morning, early.

Jonah walked back home from the pub thoughtfully. It was the first time he had done the journey sober. He stayed up with Ruby until midnight sorting through her paintings and drawings. She really was very good.

Next morning when Ruby walked into the kitchen to have her breakfast, Jonah had already been up and gone. He left her a note to say he had some business to see to. He wasn't sure when he would be back.

They were calling themselves the 'Consortium' now. Jonah and his drinking mates stood in the trainer's yard while a young girl led out the grey horse. She was a beautiful animal: if horses entered beauty contests, she would have won first prize. She knocked their socks off. Jonah had never examined a horse before, but he knew about cows. He knew what to look for. He ran his hand down the horse's front leg, looking for heat. Then lifted up her hoof and examined her metal shoe. He ran his hand along her flank and looked at her teeth. She looked in tip top condition. When he had finished, the trainer handed him the vet's report, which made Jonah's examination superfluous.

The Consortium looked at Jonah.

JONAH: 'She's fine. What are we waiting for?'

The trainer led them into her office and produced the legal papers for the transfer of ownership. They all signed on the dotted line. Jonah gave the trainer a cheque for a thousand pounds, the others did the same.

TRAINER: 'Congratulations gentlemen. You are now the proud owners of a very fine race horse. What do you want me to do with her?'

The Consortium looked at Jonah again.

JONAH: 'What do you mean 'What do you want me to do with her?'

TRAINER: 'Well, you can take her with you if you want, or she can remain here. My training fees are £200 a week.'

Jonah could have kicked himself, of course the trainer would charge them training fees. Trainers were not charities. They had to make a living like anyone else. He thought quickly.

JONAH: 'I'm a farmer. I have a paddock where I could keep her. It has a stone barn that she could use in bad weather. Next door to the paddock is a large field that has wheat in it at the moment. There is a strip of fallow land running right along the east boundary. It just needs a bit of tidying up and it would make excellent gallops. All I need is a jockey. The young girl who looks after Tulip, does she have ambitions to become a jockey?'

TRAINER: 'Oh yes, they all do. Sadly, not all of them make it.'

JONAH: 'Could I borrow her to exercise Tulip? Obviously, it would have to fit in with her work here.'

TRAINER: 'I don't see why not. To be honest I have trouble keeping her occupied. She is the daughter of one of my best clients. I only took her on to keep him happy. She is very cheap. Were you thinking of entering Tulip in races yourself?'

JONAH: 'Yes.'

TRAINER: 'You can't. You need a Trainer's licence.'

JONAH: 'Oh.'

TRAINER: 'I could enter her for you if you like. It's no skin off my nose. I take it you are planning to use Lucy as jockey.'

JONAH: 'Lucy is the young girl?'

The Trainer nodded yes.

JONAH: 'Does she have much riding experience?'

TRAINER: 'Oh yes. She has been riding all her life. It would be good experience for her. Very good experience actually. Her father will be pleased. Let's go and give her the good news.'

Lucy was overjoyed. She hugged Jonah and kissed him on both cheeks.

LUCY: 'We won't let you down, Mr Magrioni, will we, Tulip?'

The horse threw her head back and whinnied, as if she understood. She didn't, of course. She was just a horse. But animals can sense things. She would have known that something was going on, by all the attention she was getting.

JONAH: 'I'll have to get things ready for Tulip. Can you give me about a week and then I'll collect her. I have a horse box.'

TRAINER: 'Yeah, sure. And I won't even charge you.'

How did Jonah manage to work out all these things so quickly off the top of his head? He didn't work them out, He was remembering, right back to his early childhood. His father had bred race horses in the top paddock. That's why they called it the top paddock. Five acres of prime agricultural land. It had never been ploughed, at least not in Jonah's lifetime. He had been tempted to plough it a couple of times, but he never did. He couldn't really explain why. Things were coming full circle. The sheep were in them now, of course. The strip of fallow land on the east boundary of the large field that abutted the top meadow was land set aside for wildlife. The government paid Jonah to do this. The wildlife were going to have to share this strip of land with Tulip. Naughty really.

Since Ruby had been at the farm, Doris, Jonah's mother had been coming round to Sunday dinner. She used to do this when Dinah was alive. Jonah couldn't cook. If he was hungry he just sent out for a 'Belly Buster' from the local takeaway. Ruby couldn't cook either but she was learning. Dinah had an extensive collection of cookery books. Ruby was working her way through them. She made mistakes, but she was an intelligent girl and soon learned. She enjoyed cooking. They had finished their dinner: roast beef, Yorkshire puddings, roast potatoes, carrots, and peas. Ruby put on the table a strawberry cheesecake. She hadn't made it; it was frozen, from Tesco. Doris cut them each a slice. Jonah began telling them about Tulip. He was collecting her on Monday. He left out the bit about being drunk in the pub.

DORIS: 'That takes me back a bit. Vincent had horses.'

JONAH: 'I know. Where did he get them from, Mum?'

DORIS: 'He brought them with him when he came back from visiting his family in Italy, after the war. When I asked him about them, he just said they were his inheritance. He had two, a male and a female. He bred everything from those two horses. You must remember that in those days, Vincent didn't speak much English.'

Nine

With the ownership papers came Tulip's pedigree and a list of her races. The Consortium should have looked at this before they bought her but they were a bit green and were bowled over by the look of Tulip.

Tulip's mother was a grey called Candy Stripe. She hadn't done much, but her father was Dancing Boy, a famous horse. He had won several classics including the Ebor at York.

Jonah decided to look up some of his father's old racing pals. They were all pleased to see him. He hadn't seen them since Dinah's funeral. When they got onto the subject of racing, they all had a tale to tell about his father. He found he was enjoying himself. He should have done this years ago. He was too busy wallowing in his own misery. He told them about Tulip. The general opinion was that greys were not as fast as other horses. That's why they had special races for them sometimes, but they all knew Dancing Boy was a great horse.

Jonah climbed into his Land Rover and drove home. 'It could have been worse,' he thought. It didn't look like they were going to make much money out of Tulip but it surprised him that he didn't care, he was enjoying himself.

Jonah worked hard all week. He cleared out the old stone barn in the top paddock, fixed new bolts on the two stable doors and filled the area up with new bedding, putting some of the straw in the hay racks. He cut the fallow strip and baled it, stacking the bales in the barn. Finally he put up a four foot fence along the full length of the gallops. He had done it. It was probably just his imagination but he did feel as though his father was watching over him at this point.

Jonah drove into the trainer's yard on Monday morning towing his horse box behind the Land Rover. Lucy helped him load Tulip, then climbed into the passenger seat beside him. They drove off, heading for the farm. They were both a bit nervous, neither of them knew how Tulip was going to settle in. Lucy had offered to stay the night with her in the barn but Jonah wouldn't hear of it. She had done enough; he would stay with Tulip. Jonah said: 'Don't forget, we've got the sheep for company!'

Someone was tugging at Jonah's sleeve. He opened his eyes and wondered where he was. It was Tulip. He was in the stable. Jonah patted the horse's head and stood up. He had brought a bag of apples with him. He gave Tulip one. She ate it in one bite, so he gave her another one. Jonah looked at his watch, it was a quarter to six. He walked outside the barn and stretched and yawned. It was another fine, sunny morning. To his surprise, Lucy was hurrying towards him.

JONAH: 'You're an early bird!'

LUCY: 'I couldn't sleep, is she alright?'

JONAH: 'Oh yes, she's on her second apple.'

LUCY: 'Why don't you go down to the farm and get yourself a proper breakfast, Mr Magrioni. I'll look after Tulip. She can have some of this nice, fresh, grass.'

JONAH: 'OK, I'll see you later.'

When Jonah walked into the kitchen, Ruby was sat at the table eating a bowl of cornflakes.

JONAH: 'Everyone's up early this morning.'

RUBY: 'I thought I would look in at Tulip before I went to school. Would you like me to cook you some breakfast?'

JONAH: 'I would. I seem to be hungry all of a sudden. It must be sleeping in the fresh air.'

Jonah and Ruby walked back up to the top paddock. Lucy had put a saddle on Tulip and was leading her out to the gallops. She put her foot in the stirrup and climbed on board. They cantered slowly down the gallops for a while, then Lucy kicked her heels in and Tulip set off. Lucy came back smiling.

LUCY: 'I think she likes it, Mr Magrioni. I have never known her go so fast.'

Ruby joined Lucy most mornings at the gallops before she went to school. She let her have a ride on Tulip. One morning, instead of coming on her bike like she usually did, Lucy came on a handsome looking, big, black horse. His name was Rocket. He was a two year old. He was still learning. He had a tendency to run quite fast, then veer off in all directions, jumping about. Lucy had suggested to the trainer that Jonah's gallops might suit him better as they were long and thin, there was nowhere for him to run off to. The trainer agreed to try it.

Ruby Kind

Lucy sat on Rocket and Ruby sat on Tulip. Rocket set off like a rocket, leaving Tulip behind. Halfway down the gallops, he started to act up, jumping about. Tulip went past him, Rocket pricked up his ears and went after her. They finished about level then ran back. Rocket didn't mess about this time; he ran better than he had ever run. Tulip trailed in a couple of lengths behind him.

The trainer was pleased with Rocket's progress and joined Jonah on his gallops as Lucy and Ruby put the two horses through their paces. Rocket always beat Tulip, but she was getting faster.

The trainer entered Rocket in a special race at Doncaster for two year olds. He won by half a length. The trainer slipped Jonah a hundred quid in cash. Jonah put it quickly in his back pocket. He didn't tell the Consortium.

The trainer had carefully selected a race for Tulip at the same meeting. There were four horses entered for it. Tulip was in a photo finish for second, she came third. It was close. He had advised the Consortium to back the horse each way. If she came in second or third, you still got a payout. The four men trotted off happily to the bookie to collect their winnings.

Ruby Kind had their first gig: Miss Eyeball had organised a dance at the school on Saturday afternoon. The band were nervous. Ruby told them not to be; it was only a load of spotty faced kids. The gig went well. Miss Eyeball and Nathan Watterly were there. They had appointed themselves the band's unofficial managers. At the barn the following day, Nathan and Miss Eyeball went through a few things with the band that they thought they needed to work on, but on the whole, they were pleased. They asked the band if they would like to do another gig. They all said 'YES!'.

It wasn't difficult arranging more gigs. Miss Eyeball simply rang up her fellow music teachers at other schools and they organised a dance. It wasn't costing them anything and it was good fun for the kids.

They had done a couple more of these freebies when Nathan got them a paid gig at Pocklington Arts Centre. They were charging two pound on the door; a pound would go to Ruby Kind and a pound to Pocklington Arts Centre. The gig went so well the crowd wanted them back for an encore. They didn't have an encore; they had done all their songs.

Ruby Kind

So Ade Montgolfier went out and sang them a folk song. More about Ade later.

In the barn on the following day, Nathan said he was thinking of approaching Fibbers to see if he could get them a midweek gig. It would have to be midweek; the weekends were reserved for headline acts.

EVAN: 'I think we should cool it for a bit, Mr Watterly, until we have finished our GCSEs.'

MISS EYEBALL: 'He's right, Nathan. We are letting our enthusiasm run away with us. GCSEs are more important than Ruby Kind at this moment in time. I should have realised that; I'm a teacher after all. I'm sorry. What do you think, Ruby?'

RUBY: 'Well, I'm disappointed, but Evan is right. We do need to concentrate on our GCSEs but afterwards it's the school holidays. Maybe you could put together a little tour for us. What do you think, guys?'

ALL: 'GREAT!'

MISS EYEBALL: 'What do you think, Nathan? Can we put together a tour?'

NATHAN: 'No problem. I'll even borrow a van and drive you myself.'

I think it's about time I told you about Miss Eyeball. Her real name was Margaret Eye. You didn't really think she was called Miss Eyeball, did you?

She didn't know about her nickname. If she had known, she would just have laughed. She knew what kids were like. She had been one herself. When she was a little girl in junior school, they had a dinner supervisor called Mrs Brain. She was a very stern lady; no one had ever seen her smile. She used to stand watching them eat with her arms folded across her chest. If you left any of your dinner she used to tell you off. She even stood over you sometimes until you ate it. Nobody liked her. The kids had a little rhyme:

'Fee fi fo fum, this is the shape of Brainie's bum!'

They then described a large circle with their hands, and giggled.

Margaret was a graduate of the Royal Academy of Music in London, the premier music school in the country. She played the violin in the London Symphony Orchestra. She specialised in the violin but she could play most instruments. She shared a flat in Twickenham, London, with a girl called Mandy. Margaret liked to go to lectures at the British Museum. This may seem a very intellectual pursuit, but it wasn't really. The lecturers never assumed any prior knowledge; they explained things with pictures and diagrams. It was just very interesting. Last week she had gone to a lecture by an Egyptologist about how the ancient Egyptians preserved their mummies. It was incredible what they did. They removed all the internal organs, including the brain, that they dissolved by pouring liquid in the nose before they mummified it. They kept the internal organs and stored them in jars.

Tonight, Margaret was going to a lecture on Jorvik, the Viking city of York, by Dr Richard Mills of the York Archaeological Trust. She was supposed to be going with her flat mate, Mandy, but Mandy had cried off. She had bumped into an old boyfriend and he was taking her out for a meal. This often happened; Mandy changed her boyfriends like other people change their underwear, but she never fell out with them. They were always pleased to see her when they met. It was almost as though they were grateful for the little piece of her life that she had given them, they didn't expect any more.

When Mandy had answered Margaret's advert for a flat mate, she told her she was in films. Margaret said: 'You mean you're an actress?' Mandy said,: 'Yeah, sort of.' Margaret asked if she would know any of these films. Mandy smiled and said: 'I shouldn't think so.' Margaret didn't know what to make of that smile, but she didn't press the point. She wasn't the type to pry. Mandy looked a perfectly respectable girl and she was offering to pay the first month's rent in advance. Margaret offered her the room. They were mates as well as flat mates. They got on very well. Margaret considered herself lucky, you never know who you might get in London.

Mandy worked in the porn industry, but she didn't want to shock Margaret by telling her.

Margaret went to the lecture on her own. She didn't mind. She often went places on her own and people tended to talk to each other at these lectures.

Dr Richard Mills looked to be about forty. He was quite tall and had dark, curly hair, and a bushy beard. Margaret wondered what he would look like without that beard; probably ten years younger. She realised he had started speaking.

DR RICHARD: 'We started excavating in 1976. Before any development is built, particularly in York, with all its history, an archaeological dig has to be carried out. It didn't take us long to realise that we were onto something big. We were excavating find after find: Viking pottery, coins, swords, helmets. Then we got down to the buildings themselves. Very rare, they don't usually survive; they're made of wood. We hit street level, street after street. This wasn't just a few houses; it was a town. There was only one town it could be; it must be Jorvik! We were ecstatic!'

Everyone went down the pub after the lecture. Margaret found herself stood at the bar next to Dr Richard.

MARGARET: 'I really enjoyed your lecture, Doctor. I always thought Vikings were hooligans, raping and pillaging. I didn't realise they settled down and built a peaceful civilisation.'

DR RICHARD: 'Raping and pillaging went on, particularly in the early days, but that's no way to make a living. If you are going to settle somewhere, you need to build houses, plant crops, raise livestock, raise a family. Their needs were no different from ours.'

Margaret and Dr Richard managed to find a seat in the crowded pub and continued their conversation.

DR RICHARD: 'We have not only excavated Jorvik, but we have rebuilt it as well. There is a permanent exhibit underneath the Coppergate Centre in the middle of York. I can show you around if you like.'

MARGARET: 'I do hate people who make grand gestures like that, offering to do something when they have no intention of carrying it out.'

DR RICHARD: 'Whoo!'

MARGARET: 'Do you mean it? That you will show me around Jorvik?'

DR RICHARD: 'Of course.'

MARGARET: 'Are you catching the train back to York tonight?'

DR RICHARD: 'Yes. In fact, goodness, I'll have to go.'

MARGARET: 'I'll walk back with you to the station and we can see what times the trains run to York on Saturday.'

DR RICHARD: 'I do like a woman who knows her own mind. I just had a thought. We've been talking all this time about my job but I haven't a clue what you do.'

MARGARET: 'I'm a violinist with the London Symphony Orchestra.'

DR RICHARD: 'Oh my word!'

MARGARET: 'Yes, quite! You'll have to come and hear me play. But it won't be for a while. We are rehearsing for our next tour.'

DR RICHARD: 'Where is that?'

MARGARET: 'America. They love us there. Americans aren't all rap music and break dancing you know. They like their classical as well.'

Ten

Dr Richard met Margaret off the train at York station and carried her bag to his car, a battered old Saab.

DR RICHARD: 'Would you like to go round Jorvik straight away, or would you prefer a coffee at my place first?'

MARGARET: 'Coffee sounds nice.'

DR RICHARD: 'OK.'

He drove out to Claxton and parked in front of an old Methodist chapel.

MARGARET: 'Is this where you live?'

DR RICHARD: 'Yep. It's a bit basic. The estate agent described it as 'having potential'.'

Richard put his key in the door of the chapel and held it open for Margaret.

MARGARET: 'Oh, Richard, it's wonderful. I love churches.'

DR RICHARD: 'It isn't a church, it's a chapel.'

MARGARET: 'Don't be pedantic, and you have an organ.'

DR RICHARD: 'Yeah, doesn't work, I'm afraid.'

MARGARET: 'That's no problem. I know lots of people that repair organs. In fact I used one at St Mary's in Twickenham where I play the organ every Sunday when I am in London. I am not sure if they would come this far north though.'

DR RICHARD: 'No. Londoners think that Milton Keynes is up north!'

MARGARET: 'That's true, but I could always ask them. They might do it as a favour to me.'

DR RICHARD: 'I appreciate your help, Margaret, but I think there are one or two things need doing first.'

Dr Richard had lived in the chapel for about two years, but all he had done was repair the roof, put in a few kitchen units, and install a shower room and toilet. There was no central heating. It was freezing in the winter.

MARGARET: 'Yes. It looks like you are just camping out here. What you need is a push.'

DR RICHARD: 'That's true. I've had the plans drawn up. There's a mezzanine floor, 2 bedrooms, bathroom, proper kitchen, lounge. I've even got planning permission.'

MARGARET: 'What are you waiting for?'

DR RICHARD: 'I don't know really. A good woman, I suppose.'

They looked at each other. Margaret kissed him on the lips, the first time they had kissed.

MARGARET: 'I see you have only got one double bed, and it's right in front of the altar.'

DR RICHARD: 'You can have that. I'll sleep in the camp bed. It's behind that screen.'

Dr Richard had stretched a washing line across the corner of the chapel and pegged two pink sheets on it to form a screen. In the space behind the sheets was his camp bed.

MARGARET: 'Mmm, very ingenious. I wonder how long that will last.'

DR RICHARD: 'I'll put the kettle on.'

He filled the electric kettle with water and switched it on. Then he fetched a cafetiere and spooned in two tablespoons of Kenyan, ground coffee. Margaret was sat on an old blue sofa that Dr Richard had got from a charity shop. It was the only seat in the chapel. Richard handed her her coffee.

MARGARET: 'Mmm, this is good.'

They sat for a while in silence, drinking.

MARGARET: 'I should have known you wouldn't live somewhere ordinary.'

DR RICHARD: 'I couldn't afford to live somewhere ordinary. I got this place cheap. This tour of yours to America, when does it start?'

MARGARET: 'In about three weeks' time.'

DR RICHARD: 'We had better make the most of it then. Can I crash down on your sofa next weekend?'

MARGARET: 'I don't see why not. I warn you, though, I share the flat with a beautiful blond girl called Mandy. She likes to walk around in the nude.'

DR RICHARD: 'I'll just have to grin and bear it.'

They finished their coffee and set off in the Saab for York and the Jorvik Viking centre.

I won't say too much about the Jorvik Viking Centre. I don't want to spoil your enjoyment if you decide to visit.

Margaret and Dr Richard carried on a long distance romance for a couple of years, during which time, they converted the chapel into a comfortable home, sharing the cost. Margaret then fell pregnant. The pregnancy pushed her further in a direction that she was already heading. She liked playing with the Orchestra but she was growing tired of the travelling. She talked it over with Dr Richard and decided to move into the chapel. Before she did this, Dr Richard put an advert for her in The Press, offering her services as a music teacher, including lessons on the church organ. The advert attracted half a dozen replies from people wanting lessons, plus a couple of replies from schools who didn't have a music teacher.

Margaret soon settled into a routine and her list of clients grew.

After baby Paul was born, Margaret continued to work from home until he turned three years old. She and Dr Richard had discussed it and they thought that Paul was ready to attend nursery. They looked at a few nurseries and settled on one in Castlegate. What had set this off was the up-and-coming vacancy at the Joseph Rowntree School. Margaret taught advanced violin to some of the pupils there in the sixth form, a couple of hours, once a week. The full time music teacher was retiring and she had recommended Margaret as her replacement, but the headmaster's hands were tied. He couldn't just give the job to Margaret. She would have to apply for it along with everyone else. It was a farce. Margaret had a dream CV: a first class Honours Degree from the London School of Music and five years as a violinist with the London Symphony Orchestra, plus her uncanny ability to play most other instruments, from the trombone to the church organ. She was head and shoulders above the other applicants. They would be fools not to offer her the job.

They offered her the job. Dr Richard said they would.

Margaret enjoyed teaching the kids. They constantly amazed her. Ruby Fish was a prodigious talent. She enjoyed her role as Ruby Kind's unofficial joint manager with Nathan Watterly. It gave her a buzz like the live performances with the orchestra used to do. Nathan often kept them all entertained with his tales of life on the road. Margaret had a few of these tales herself, but Nathan's were spectacular, especially the early ones in the sixties. Even then, she suspected that he watered them down for the sake of his young audience.

They were all sat round in the barn having finished rehearsing some new songs that Ruby had arranged: Ruby Kind, Miss Eyeball and Nathan Watterly.

Nathan was telling them about the early days in the sixties with The Bloggs.

NATHAN: 'Our manager was a pub landlord called Eric Freebody. He was the chairman of the local Licensed Victuallers Association. He knew all the local landlords in North London. We played in most of the pubs in north London. We had an old Ford Transit van with a bench seat in the front. Our gear went in the back and we all piled in the front. There were four of us. I was the only one who had passed the test so I had to drive. We couldn't afford an overnight stop in a hotel after the gig so I drove back, through the deserted streets of London, in the early hours of the morning, desperately trying to keep my eyes open whilst the others snored their heads off next to me.

Eric had excelled himself. Somehow he managed to get us a gig supporting The Bones. To this day, I don't know how he did it, but it was in Brighton. Too far for us to drive back so we would need an overnight stop.

Eric rang Andy, The Bones' manager. He said not to worry, he would book us into the same hotel as The Bones. It wouldn't cost us anything. There were a lot of girls in the hotel. We called them groupies, but I don't think they all were. Quite a lot

Ruby Kind

of them were just local girls. Groupies are girls that follow the bands around. Some of the girls were wandering up and down the corridors stark naked. When they couldn't find a bone, they moved onto us. And that is all I'm going to tell you.

EVAN: 'Aww, come on, Nathan. You're just getting to the juicy bit.'

The others joined in the furore. Nathan held up his hands.

NATHAN: 'No, I'm not telling you anything else; you're too young.'

Eleven

Ruby and the band had taken their GCSEs. It was the start of the long summer holidays. Nathan and Miss Eyeball had put together a tour for them that would see them playing twice a week for the whole summer. All paid gigs.

True to his word, Nathan had borrowed a van and Ruby was sat next to him in the passenger seat, heading for their first gig at Saltburn church hall. The rest of the band followed behind in Miss Eyeball's car.

The vicar said it would be a young audience, plus a few mums and dads doing the refreshments. So Ruby had decided to start with a teeny bopper number called Beach Ball.

The church hall was packed. Ruby Kind set up their instruments and did a sound check. They didn't expect everyone to be here so early. The crowd joined in with the sound check. When they were ready to start, the vicar stepped up to the microphone.

VICAR: 'Tap, tap tap. Testing, testing.'

Ruby Kind

VOICE IN THE CROWD: 'We've done the sound check.'

VICAR: 'Oh, sorry. Right then. I want you to give a really big Saltburn welcome to a very exciting band that have come all the way from York. Ladies and gentlemen, boys and girls, I give you Ruby Kind.'

The crowd cheered and clapped. Ruby Kind launched into Beach Ball. Ruby and Kirsty took lead vocals.

Like a beach ball, beach ball
My heart's a bumping, Like a beach ball, beach ball
My heart's a bumping Like a beach ball, beach ball
My heart's a bumping, thumping,
When I hold you in my arms

My Mumma says I'm just another teenage girl
With a crush upon a boy at school
But I don't know, I can't explain, my head's in a whirl
I get hungry when I think of you

A shoo shoo pop, a shoo, shoo pop
A shoo shoo pop, a shoo, shoo pop
A shoo shoo pop, a shoo, shoo pop, A yeah, yeah, yeah
A shoo shoo pop, a shoo, shoo pop
A shoo shoo pop, a shoo, shoo pop

A shoo shoo pop, a shoo, shoo pop,
A shoo shoo pop, a shoo, shoo pop

I met you out of school, remember our first kiss
Sent a shiver up and down my spine
I'm grinning like a fool, I'm happy all of the time
When I'm walking with your hand in mine

CHORUS 1

CHORUS 2

Like a beach ball, beach ball, My heart's a bumping
Like a beach ball, beach ball, My heart's a bumping
Like a beach ball, beach ball, My heart's a bumping, thumping
When I hold you in a my
When I hold you in a my
When I hold you in a my arms, yeah
When I hold you in a my arms, whoo

The crowd wouldn't let them go. The band had agreed that if they got an encore, they would do Whopper. Jason had even brought his xylophone. When the hubbub finally died down, Ruby explained the story behind Whopper and rehearsed the audience for their verse. Jason hit the big bass drum and they were off.

Ruby Kind

Everyone agreed that it had been a good night. The vicar was well pleased. He said he would definitely book them again. He asked Ruby where he could get a copy of Whopper. He wanted to play it to his mother and toddler group. He thought it would help with potty training. Ruby said she would burn him a copy, whatever that meant.

The following morning, Sunday, Ruby was in the barn looking through Jonah's records. She had doubled the band's number of songs to 24 but it was obvious from the Saltburn gig that they needed more.

York had their very own famous punk band called 'Puke'. Their debut album: 'Puke your guts out' went to number one and sold over a million copies. They were awarded a gold disc.

Puke were due to embark on their first US tour in about three weeks' time. Rupert Spithead, the band's lead singer and songwriter was driving from York to Hull to see his parents. As usual, he was driving too fast.

He was up the boot of a couple of old farts in front, tooting his horn. The old folks were shocked at the aggression and slowed down. Rupert gave them the V sign and pulled out to overtake. Unfortunately, he didn't look where he was going. He was right on a bend and ploughed headlong into a car coming the other way.

The driver of the other car was killed instantly, but the firemen managed to cut Rupert out of the wreckage alive; only just. The Yorkshire Air Ambulance helicopter took Rupert to Hull Royal Infirmary where surgeons operated on his brain for five hours. Rupert had broken both legs, a couple of ribs, and his right wrist. But by far the worst injury was to his head. He had a fractured skull and quite a deep puncture wound to his brain.

Afterwards, the surgeon told Rupert's parents that he thought he would live but there was a strong possibility that he would have brain damage. Rupert was in a coma for about six weeks. When he finally did wake up, he could remember nothing of the accident.

Puke never did go on their tour of America. Rupert recovered, his voice was the same, but it was like a light had gone out in his head and he was groping about in the dark. The aggression that characterised their music had gone; their act was a parody of what it was before the accident. But Rupert clung to the band like a limpet. It was all he lived for. It was the only thing that kept him going. Without it he thought he might die. They played 3 or 4 gigs a month, booked mostly by venues that remembered the old Puke. Everyone hoped that one day Rupert would wake up and be his old self. Sometimes he would have flashes of his old self, but it was elusive, like trying to catch a butterfly. Puke only kept going for Rupert's sake. They all had other jobs except Rupert who was on Incapacity Benefit and Disability Living Allowance.

Ruby and Jonah listened to one side of the Sex Pistols record all the way through.

RUBY: 'I wonder if we dare do any of it.'

JONAH: 'I don't see why not. So long as you don't put a safety pin through your nose. Aileen wouldn't be too happy about that.'

Jonah was reading 'What's on' in The Press, a summary of all the entertainment in York and the surrounding area for the week ahead. He was looking for somewhere to go with Rhonda. They had been going out for quite a while now, but they were as different as chalk and cheese. Rhonda liked dancing and the theatre. Jonah liked long country walks and going down the pub. They only carried on seeing each other because they were both lonely.

Ruby was reading a book about the French Revolution.

JONAH: 'Hallo! Puke are playing at Fibbers on Wednesday night. Do you fancy going?'

Ruby hadn't told Ruby Kind about her interest in punk. She didn't know how they would react. But she hadn't given up on it.

RUBY: 'Certainly do!'

JONAH: 'Somehow I don't think it would be Rhonda's cup of tea.'

Wednesday was a quiet night at Fibbers. Ruby and Jonah got there at about 9 o'clock. Puke were due on at ten. A group of about twenty punks were gathered in front of the stage.

The DJ was playing a Boom Town Rats record: 'I don't like Mondays'.

JONAH: 'Feels like a wake.'

Ruby Kind

RUBY: 'What's a wake? ... Only joking.'

They sat at the back of the club. Jonah had a pint of shandy and Ruby had a coke.

About half past nine a group of women came in. It looked like a hen party. One of the women had balloons tied all over her and a large L plate fastened on her back. They were all giggling, one or two were unsteady on their feet. They had obviously been drinking.

JONAH: 'At least they liven the place up a bit.'

RUBY: 'I never like to see women drunk. I always think they are so vulnerable.'

JONAH: 'You put me to shame, Ruby. It amazes me how you have turned out so well.'

After a few more punk records, the DJ walked onto the stage and said in a flat voice, as if he were reading the shipping forecast: 'Ladies and Gentlemen, will you please welcome the legend that is Puke.'

The band ambled onto the stage. They were dressed in their punk gear, but they all had conventional haircuts, except for Rupert Spithead who had a glorious, spikey, pink Mohican over six inches tall. He really looked every inch a punk. The group of punks out the front cheered and Puke blasted out their first song: 'Bolux'.

I'm talking bolux, we're talking bolux
You're talking bolux, and you're listening to me
I'm talking bolux, we're talking bolux
You're talking bolux, and you're listening to me

I'm going home to make my bed
I'm going home to rest my head
I'm going home and that's no lie
Wasting my time

I'm going home to brush my teeth
I'm going home to get some relief
I'm going home to scratch my ass
Making it last

Repeat complete

It sounded as though it had once been a decent song, but Rupert sang it with no emotion in his voice. He face was like a mask. During the instrumental parts he stood stock still, gazing out above the small crowd with a thousand yard stare.

They carried onto the next song. Rupert didn't talk to the audience. To the left of Rupert was a woman in a white dress. She didn't look like she belonged there. In fact, she looked like a bride at a wedding.

She sang backing vocals. She was Sadie, Rupert's girlfriend. The next song they sang was: 'Shit on my Shoe.'

> *I got shit on my shoe, Waiting for you*
> *I been waiting so long, Wondering what's wrong*
> *I got shit on my shoe, Waiting for you*
> *I been waiting so long, Wondering what's wrong*
> *Widge you, I got shit on my shoe*

> *Where have you bin, Why don't you ring*
> *Pick up the phone, Don't leave me alone*
> *Where have you bin, Why don't you ring*
> *Pick up the phone, Don't leave me alone*
> *Widge you, why don't you pick up the phone*

Sadie on vocals

> *The leaves are brown,*
> *The wind it blows them all around*
> *The sky is grey,*
> *The wind it blows the clouds away*

> *You stood me up, You don't give a fuck*
> *You broke my heart, You made me fart*
> *You stood me up, You don't give a fuck*
> *You broke my heart, You made me fart*
> *Widge you, you broke my heart*
> *I got shit on my shoe, Waiting for you*
> *I been waiting so long, Wondering what's wrong*

Paul Philip Studer

*I got shit on my shoe, Waiting for you
I been waiting so long, Wondering what's wrong*

Widge you, I got shit on my shoe

Repeat verse

Puke only played for about half an hour, there was no encore. Ruby abandoned her brief flirtation with punk. To make it sound convincing you needed a kind of raw aggression. Without it, it sounded a bit silly.

Twelve

Ruby and Jonah had traced the Magrioni family tree back to Pisa in Italy, but when Ruby logged onto the Italian website, it was in Italian, obviously. Neither she nor Jonah spoke Italian. Ruby bought an English/Italian dictionary and began painstakingly translating the information on the website. She had a bit of success. She found a Paolo Magrioni who lived on a farm on the outskirts of Pisa. She discussed it with Jonah and they decided to write Paolo a letter. It was a bit of a long shot. There were three Magrionis in Pisa but Doris said that Vincent's family definitely lived on a farm somewhere in the countryside around Pisa. Of the other two Magrionis, one was a butcher with an address in the centre of Pisa and the other was a judge, all of 85 years old.

Ruby and Jonah wrote the letter in English, putting in everything they knew about their family tree. Jonah was all for sending the letter as it was, but Ruby knew she must translate it into Italian if they were to stand any chance of interesting Paolo. Ruby wished she knew someone who spoke Italian. She even went to an Italian Restaurant in Walmgate to see if the owner could help her but he said he came from Bolton and his waiters were from Bangladesh. There was nothing for it, she would have to translate the letter herself. It would take some time. She had just about finished the translation when she got a call from the Italian Restaurant Manager, Wally. He had taken her phone number and said he would ring her if he found someone who could help her. A young Italian language student called Maria had come to work for him. She would happily translate Ruby's letter for her.

Ruby got on her bike and pedalled into town. She got off her bike and rang the restaurant bell. It was shut. Wally, the manager, opened the door and wheeled Ruby's bike into the restaurant.

WALLY: 'If you leave it there, it will be gone by the time you get back.'

Wally introduced Ruby to Maria, the young Italian girl. Ruby gave her her original English letter and her Italian translation. Maria laughed.

MARIA: 'This is the worst Italian I have ever seen!'

Ruby blushed.

MARIA: 'I am so sorry. I should not have said that. You try your best. I will translate this tomorrow morning. You can pick it up at lunchtime. I am working tonight. Tomorrow morning will be the first opportunity I will have.'

RUBY: 'Thank you so much, Maria. I really appreciate it.'

Ruby tried to give Maria some money, but she wouldn't take it.

WALLY: 'Come and have a meal with us. Bring your Uncle. I will cook you the best Italian meal you have ever had.'

RUBY: 'Thank you both so much. You have been very kind. We would love to come for a meal.'

Ruby collected the translation the next day and booked a meal for herself and Jonah in the evening.

Ruby took the letter to the Post Office and asked for it to be sent Air Mail to Italy. The Post mistress put on the stamp and said she would see it went off today. That was it. There was nothing more to do except wait.

Paolo was curious about the letter from England. He didn't know anyone from England. He slit open the letter with a kitchen knife and read it. He put the letter down on the kitchen table, scratched his head, and read it again. It was unbelievable; if it was true, that is. The letter had obviously been written by an Italian person but it was signed by Ruby Fish, an English name. Paolo sat for a while, wondering what to do. Then he rang his sister, Sophia.

Sophia was sat in the observation gallery at the Holy Spirit Hospital watching an operation. She was studying to be a doctor there. She was twenty, in her third year. She was actually on her summer holidays at the moment, but she liked to use the time to watch as many operations as she could. She wanted to become a surgeon, but was keeping an open mind about what to specialise in. Her mobile phone rang. She went outside and along the corridor to the lift lobby and answered it.

SOPHIA: 'Hallo, Paolo. Is everything alright? You don't normally ring me at this time.'

Sophia had caller ID on her phone. Paolo's name had come up on the screen.

PAOLO: 'I've had this amazing letter, Sophia. I can hardly believe it. We may have relatives in England! I had to call you.'

SOPHIA: 'Calm down, Paolo and tell me what the letter says.'

PAOLO: 'I can't read it all. It's too long. It's written by someone called Ruby Fish, but her Uncle is called Jonah Magrioni and his father was called Vincent Magrioni. He was a prisoner of war in Yorkshire during the Second World War. It fits, Sophia. Vincent could be Grandad's brother. He would be the right age.'

SOPHIA: 'I must see this letter. But I can't come today, I have to watch the operation.'

PAOLO: 'Oh no. Did they hear your phone ring?'

SOPHIA: 'It's alright. I had it on vibrate. No one noticed. I'm stood in the lift lobby at the moment.'

PAOLO: 'What kind of operation is it?'

SOPHIA: 'It's a heart transplant.'

PAOLO: 'I didn't know the Holy Spirit did heart transplants.'

SOPHIA: 'They don't normally. This is the first. That's why I have to see it. Look Paolo, I don't know how long this operation is going to take, then there will be a debrief with the surgeon afterwards. It could be late. I'll catch the train first thing tomorrow morning and be with you about nine.'

PAOLO: 'Ok, sis, Ciao!'

Sophia went back to the viewing gallery. The surgeon had opened the man's chest cavity and was cutting the breast bone.

Jonah and Ruby were late up. It was Saturday morning. Ruby Kind had played at Fibbers last night, late. They were the main act on Friday night. Bert Walkman, the manager of Fibbers, had rung Nathan in a panic. He had been let down by the Drumbeats who were his headline act on Friday night, one of the busiest nights of the week. The Drumbeats had had their van stolen with all their gear in it. They had pulled into a service station at Leicester Forest East for a bite to eat. When they came back, the van was gone.

Kevin, the Drumbeats keyboard player rang Lenny Ravowich, their manager. Lenny was already in York. He had gone ahead to see someone about another gig. He cursed when Kevin told him what had happened and quickly set about organising transport to get the group back to London. For a couple of minutes, he racked his brains trying to think were he could get some replacement gear, but it was too late. He was running out of time. He decided to go and see Bert in person rather than

Ruby Kind

ring him. It was the least he could do. Fibbers was an important gig, a regular gig. He didn't want to lose it.

Ruby Kind had been booked to play at Fibbers on Wednesday night in about 3 weeks' time. Bert asked Nathan if they could step in and take the Drumbeats' place. Then he mentioned a figure that, when Nathan told Ruby, she couldn't believe.

Ruby Kind were rehearsing in the barn. They had a gig on Saturday night and another on Sunday. They were trying out a couple of new numbers. Jonah came running in and interrupted them.

JONAH: 'Nathan is on the phone Ruby. I think it's the big one.'

Ruby rushed out to the phone. She came back and gave the band the news.

RUBY: 'Get your things together, guys. We've got a gig. We are the headline act at Fibbers – TONIGHT!'

They didn't have time to be nervous. Jonah brought Rhonda. Margaret came with Dr Richard. Jonah rang Aileen and Maurice but they couldn't come, they were playing bridge with one of their neighbours. Nathan brought the van round and they loaded up the gear.

Lenny stayed to see Ruby Kind. Bert said he was in for a treat. 'They're good', thought Lenny, 'not professional standard, obviously, but not far off'. He particularly liked their modern take on pop classics, not unlike the Drumbeats. They played a couple of songs that Lenny hadn't heard in a long time: 'I'm not in Love' and 'If you leave me now'. The songs were diametrically opposed; one was about a man telling his girlfriend that he was not in love, and the other was about a man pleading with his girlfriend not to leave him. Lenny wondered if this was intentional. When he asked Ruby about it after the show, she said it was, but he was the only one that had noticed it. That was clever, very clever. Ade sang in his clear, strong voice.

Thirteen

Jonah walked into the kitchen to get his breakfast. Ruby was there before him. She was getting eggs and bacon out of the fridge.

RUBY: 'Eggs and bacon, Uncle Jonah?'

JONAH: 'Yes, please Ruby, thank you. I do appreciate you being here, Ruby. I haven't said that before, have I. I should have done.'

RUBY: 'At least you notice I am here Uncle Jonah and you talk to me like a real person. At home, I'm invisible. I think Mum and Dad just forget I'm there. They only notice me when I am an inconvenience to them when I'm ill or something. All they do then is ring Gran and leave her to look after me.'

JONAH: 'Yes, Aileen always was self-centred. She is about three years older than me. She would never play with me when we were kids. She preferred playing with her dolls. She spent hours playing with her dolls; she had loads of them. She gave them all names. She even made little clothes for them. She talked to them and they answered back. Aileen changed her voice for every doll. It's amazing how she did that.

I remember it was a lovely sunny day and I wanted someone to play with. I must have been about six or seven. I was on my swing, trying to go backwards and forwards. What I needed was a push. I ran upstairs and into Aileen's bedroom and asked her to come out to play. She ignored me at first, then she replied in one of her doll's voices: 'We are having a tea party, don't interrupt.'

I slammed the bedroom door and ran down the stairs crying. Mum called us in for tea. When we were all sat at the table, this kitchen table in fact, me, Aileen, Mum, and Dad, I said I wanted to go to the toilet and ran upstairs. I went in Aileen's bedroom and threw all her dolls out of the bedroom window. Then I calmly went downstairs and ate my tea.

Aileen always washed up. She was very domesticated. When she had finished, she went up to her bedroom and SCREAMED. She screamed and screamed and screamed, real, wild, uncontrollable screams. Mum and Dad rushed upstairs to see what was the matter. Aileen was incoherent. She screamed and shouted and pointed to all her dolls laid on the back grass outside. She actually frothed at the mouth. I knew that cos I poked my head round the bedroom door.

Mum and Dad did all they could to try and calm her down. But she just carried on screaming. In the end, Mum called the doctor. He came and gave her something to calm her down. They gave her two more pills after the doctor had gone. Eventually she slept.

Mum and Dad were shaken. We all sat back down at this kitchen table. No one said anything. Finally, I could stand it no longer and blurted out:

JONAH: 'I couldn't help it, Mum. She will never play with me. I've tried everything. I've been nice to her, I've talked to her about her dolls, I even offered her Peter Rabbit, my favourite toy. She said she didn't want him; he was too scruffy. I just wanted to get through to her. Throwing her dolls out the window was the only thing that I thought would get a reaction.'

DORIS: 'You were right there, son.'

Silence again.

DORIS: 'If you want someone to play with you, Jonah, come and see me. I'll play with you. I can't promise to run round the garden with you all the time, but I'll certainly push you on your swing and you can come in the kitchen here with me and we can do some baking. I'll show you how to make jam tarts. You like jam tarts, don't you?'

Jonah nodded.

Vincent held up his finger.

VINCENT: 'You can come and help me on the farm. I will teach you to ride horse.'

DORIS: 'Are you sure, Vincent? Samson and Delilah are very big.'

VINCENT: 'I will buy small horse.'

DORIS: 'You mean a pony.'

VINCENT: 'Si, pony.'

DORIS: 'Can we afford a pony, Vincent?'

VINCENT: 'I will do this for my son,'

Vincent struck his chest with his hand. What he lacked in English, he made up for with hand gestures.

A week later, Dad drove into the yard towing the horse box. He waved me over. I was watching from the window.

VINCENT: 'Open door, Jonah.'

I opened the door of the horse box and there, looking at me, was the most beautiful Shetland pony with her long mane and big brown eyes. I fell in love instantly. Goodness knows where he got her from. Dad knew lots of horsey people.

From then on, Aileen and me went our separate ways. We only spoke to each other when we had to.'

RUBY: 'Wow!'

JONAH: 'I've never told anyone that story before.'

RUBY: 'It explains a lot.'

The phone rang. Ruby got up and answered it. She was amazed to be talking to someone called Sophia Magrioni, who said she might be her long lost Italian cousin! Ruby waved Jonah over quickly, told him who she was talking to, and held the receiver a little way off her ear so that Jonah could hear.

SOPHIA: 'We got your letter. We had no idea we had any family in England. Unfortunately, my grandfather died about five years ago. He never said anything about his family. I should have asked him, I suppose, but I was only fifteen. I was more interested in boys than family history. Then he died and it was too late.'

RUBY: 'Uncle Jonah wants a word.'

JONAH: 'Hallo, Sophia. My dad died about ten years ago. He was a lovely man. He taught me how to ride a horse. I used to help him on the farm. He told me a bit about his family in Italy, how they had a farm there and also how they bred horses. Most of what I know I got from my mother. She has given me a tin full of old photographs. I don't know any of the people in the photographs. They are taken in vineyards, olive groves, wheat fields, there are pictures of men holding horses. I would love to know if you can shed any light on them.'

SOPHIA: 'We still breed horses, and we have a vineyard, and an olive grove. They could be from the farm here. I would love to see them. Just a minute, Paolo is saying something. I'm afraid he doesn't speak English.

He says he is looking forward to seeing you.

Actually, that's not a bad idea. Why don't you fly over and see us. We've got plenty of room at the farmhouse. You can stay as long as you like, have a holiday.'

JONAH: 'I'd love to. Oh, there's a problem, here's Ruby.'

RUBY: 'I'm in a band, Sophia. We've got gigs every weekend during the summer holidays, but I could make it during the week if that's ok. Uncle Jonah is nodding.'

SOPHIA: 'Yes, please!' Sophia laughed. 'Paolo has just punched the air. He is running around as if he has scored a goal!'

The plane touched down at Pisa airport, just gone twelve noon on Monday morning. Ruby and Jonah walked down the steps. The heat hit them. A heat haze hung over the tarmac. Outside the terminal building, a row of taxis waited. Ruby and Jonah climbed into the back of one of them and gave the driver the address of Paolo and Sophia's farm. The journey took ten minutes. They could have walked it.

Paolo and Sophia greeted them with open arms. Paolo led the way through the kitchen and onto a paved courtyard out the back. Above the courtyard was a pergola, hung with grapes. In the middle was a large old table and chairs, groaning with food.

RUBY: 'Good grief, Sophia. How many are you expecting?'

Sophia laughed.

SOPHIA: 'I've been cooking ever since you put the phone down.'

Paolo said something in Italian.

SOPHIA: 'He says he has been starving for the last two days. I wouldn't let him eat anything.'

They all laughed at that.

Paolo poured them each a glass of wine and they tucked in. Everything that Ruby tried was delicious. Sophia and Paolo wanted to see Jonah's photographs. He produced the original Ringtons Tea tin that Doris had given him and took off the lid. He took out photographs and handed them round. One of the photographs was of four young men. They were stood in a cornfield.

JONAH: 'By the looks of the horses and the old fashioned farm machinery, I'd say this was taken before the war.'

None of them recognised the men. They looked at more of the photos. Paolo said they all looked to have been taken at the farm. He recognised the vineyard and the olive groves and some of the farm buildings, but none of them recognised any of the faces. It was hardly surprising. The photographs were taken over sixty years ago. People change a lot in 60 years.

Sophia suggested they clear the table so that they could lay the photographs out. They played a game a bit like 'Patience' in cards, placing all the similar faces together. As well as the four men, there were several photos of an older couple which Sophia took to be their mother's mother and father, plus numerous pictures of people gathering in the harvest, including children.

They were nearing the bottom of the tin when Jonah said: 'Got it!' He was looking at a photograph, obviously taken a lot later than the others, judging by the clothes, of two men holding a horse. Jonah pointed to one of the men.

JONAH: 'That's Dad. That's Vincent.'

Paolo looked at the photo and grinned. He pointed to the other man and said: 'Luigi'. The other man was Paolo and Sophia's grandad.

JONAH: 'I think I even recognise the horse. It looks a lot like Samson. It must have been taken when Vincent visited his family in Italy after the war. He actually brought two horses back with him, put them on the train!'

Sophia picked up the old photograph of the four men, taken before the war and placed it above the more recent photograph of Vincent and Luigi with the horse. Her training in medicine had taught her to observe people closely. Doctors learn a lot just by looking at people. She focused on the men's faces, looking at their bone structure, the shape of their nose and mouth, their eyes. These things changed very little over the years.

All conversation had stopped. They knew what Sophia was doing. Eventually, she tapped two of the men in the old photograph with her finger.

SOPHIA: 'That's Vincent and that's Luigi. The other two have certain facial similarities. They could be brothers, but you often get common features with people from a certain area. They might just be farm labourers.'

Jonah sat back in his chair and blew out his cheeks.

JONAH: 'That's it! That proves it. We are all family!'

The others had realised the same thing. They laughed, clapped, and hugged each other. Then Jonah put his foot in it.

JONAH: 'When are we going to meet your mother and father then?'

There was an embarrassed silence. Sophia said something in Italian to Paolo. Brother and sister looked at each other. Ruby looked at Jonah, Jonah shrugged as if to say: 'What have I said?'

Fourteen

SOPHIA: 'I think we should go inside. I will explain.'

Sophia led them into the lounge and they all sat down. Then she started telling them the terrible story of the storm.

SOPHIA: 'Mum and Dad, Mum's mum and dad and Dad's mum and dad had been talking about sailing around the Greek Islands for years, only this year, they were actually going to do it. They had hired a boat called Ulysses II for a month and had fixed on a date of June 10th. Both Grandads had been fishermen in their younger days and Dad sailed regularly in his neighbour's boat. Dad assumed the role of skipper.

They set out from Athens on a beautiful sunny morning. Me and Paolo waved them off. They all waved back, except Dad; he was at the wheel. We heard from them regularly, postcards from the various islands that they visited and the occasional phone call.

It was Tuesday night on the third week of the trip, when a storm blew up. No one knows what happened. The coastguard said they must have been anchored off Paros. He received a mayday call from them at 11.37 at night. They tried but they couldn't launch the lifeboat; the sea was too rough. They waited an agonising three hours, then the crew managed to get the lifeboat out. The sea was still rough but they were determined to go.

They knew the position that the mayday call had been sent from by the GPS. They searched the area but couldn't find anything. The lifeboat had big searchlights but it was difficult searching in the dark. After a couple of hours, they decided to come back at daybreak.

They resumed their search at first light. The sea was calm, there was nothing to show of the night's mayhem; no boat, no wreckage, nothing. Reluctantly, they called off the search. Two of the lifeboat men were divers. They came back after work, in their own time and dived at the site of the search. Again, they found nothing, but they didn't give up. They came back every evening and continued searching.

After three weeks, one of the divers spotted an anchor chain. He followed it and there was Ulysses II lying on her side, with her back broken. The divers marked the position with a buoy and reported their find to the coastguard.

The coastguard rang us with the news. He asked me what I wanted him to do. He said he couldn't raise the boat as it was in two pieces. Did we want him to look inside for bodies. I couldn't think of my parents and grandparents as bodies. The coastguard sensed my difficulties and said, kindly, that he thought they had better have a look and to leave it to them. I didn't appreciate why he said this at the time. We were supposed to pay for the recovery, but I didn't realise that until our neighbour told us, the one that Dad used to go sailing with. When I offered to pay, the coastguard wouldn't take anything. He said the divers didn't want paying; they had been profoundly affected by the tragedy. They wanted to help; they didn't do it for money.

The divers brought up both sets of grandparents but there was no sign of Mum and Dad. They have never been found.'

Silence settled on the room like a heavy blanket, then Ruby began to cry. She set off Sophia, soon they were all roaring.

Paolo poured them each a brandy. Ruby had never had brandy before. She tentatively sipped the fiery liquid, feeling it burn all the way down.

JONAH: 'Me and my big mouth.'

SOPHIA: 'Don't blame yourself, Jonah. It had to be told. You had to know. I feel better now it's out in the open.'

There was a loud knock on the back door. Paolo got up and answered it. He came rushing back, said something in rapid Italian to Sophia, and rushed out.

SOPHIA: 'One of the mares is giving birth. He has to go.'

RUBY: 'Can we have a look?'

SOPHIA: 'Of course!'

The mare was struggling. She had been in labour for over an hour. Paolo inserted his hand and had a feel around. He said something in Italian.

SOPHIA: 'He thinks the foal is the wrong way round.'

Jonah, who had some experience of difficult births in sheep and cows, offered to have a look. He took off his shirt, soaped his arm and pushed it as far as he could into the horse's womb. Slowly he felt around, he could feel the feet, the head, but they were trapped by the umbilical cord. Gently, he eased the cord clear and pulled the foal. It came out all in a rush. Paolo was overjoyed. He actually kissed Jonah; very Italian, you don't get that in Yorkshire.

They were all sat on bales of straw watching the new-born foal.

JONAH: 'Life goes on, Sophia. No matter what happens, life goes on.

SOPHIA: 'Me and Paolo thought we were alone in the world, that we had no family left. When we received your letter, we couldn't believe it. We wanted it to be true but we had no means of proving it. Now we have, the feeling is indescribable.'

RUBY: 'You will have to come and see us in York. Come and see me in the band.'

SOPHIA: 'Yes. I want to hear all about this band. In fact, I want to hear all about everything. We have only just begun. I think there is more to discover in the Magrioni family tree. Will you look on the website with me, Ruby. I want to learn how to use it so I can trace our ancestors back further. We may have even more relatives that we don't know about.

RUBY: 'Yes, of course. I'd love to show you. I don't think I can get much further myself, not unless I take a crash course in Italian.'

JONAH: 'Will you ask Paolo, Sophia, how many horses he has.'

Through his sister, Paolo explained about his pride and joy.

PAOLO: 'I've got four brood mares, including this one. One is pregnant and the other two have had their foals and are ready to be mated again. I have one stud stallion and two more stallions that I race. Both the racing stallions have won races but Titian is the best. He has won many races. He is running again on Saturday at Societa Alfea Spa if you would like to see him.'

JONAH: 'I would love to. Do you mind going home on your own, Ruby? I would really love to stay and see Titian run.'

RUBY: 'I think I can just about manage that Uncle Jonah. I'm a big girl now.'

They all laughed at that.

Ruby and Sophia left the two men in the barn, went inside, and switched on the computer. They logged onto the Ancestry website and looked up Vincent and Luigi's birth certificates. There were two more birth certificates listed for the Magrioni family: Giorgio and Luca. The four men in the old photograph were indeed brothers.

SOPHIA: 'I think they must have died. I don't remember them when I was growing up.'

RUBY: 'We'll have a look for their death certificates.'

They found them. Giorgio and Luca Magrioni both died on 18 March 1944.

RUBY: 'Mmm, 1944. That would be the battle of Monte Cassino.'

SOPHIA: 'How do you know that?'

RUBY: 'I'm reading about the second world war. What we need is their Army records. Have you any idea where the Italian Army records are kept?'

SOPHIA: 'I haven't got a clue.'

RUBY: 'We'll Google them.'

Ruby brought up the Google search engine and Sophia typed in Italian: 'The Italian Army records'.

Italian records are kept at local level. They found them at Pisa Town Hall. Ruby and Sophia met the Town Clerk. He couldn't have been more helpful.

Ruby was right. Both Giorgio and Luca had died at the Battle of Monte Cassino. They also found out that Vincent had been wounded at the same battle and captured by the British. He had been shot in the lung.

Reluctantly, Ruby had to leave it there. She was playing tomorrow night in Sheffield with Ruby Kind and had to fly back home.

SOPHIA: 'Not to worry. I think I've got the hang of it now. I'll carry on. Something tells me I won't be watching too many operations this summer. What is your email address, Ruby? I'll write to you with anything I find out and you can help me if I get stuck.'

Paolo and Jonah didn't speak each other's language but they had developed a kind of understanding. They communicated by gestures and facial expressions, plus a few words that they had learned from each other. They got on very well.

They were stood in the stands at Societa Alfea Spa, their binoculars trained on the starting gate that Titian had just entered. The gate went up and they were off. Titian settled down in the middle of the pack. Paolo gave Jonah the thumbs up, Jonah smiled. He had put the equivalent of 100 pounds on Titian to win. The big, black horse eased his way through the field. Jonah watched as they came into the finishing straight. The jockey hit Titian with his whip and he moved up to second place. Another whip and Titian crossed the line half a length in front. Paolo and Jonah shouted in their respective languages and hugged each other.

Titian had been the favourite so the odds were not very good. Even so, they had each made a tidy profit. Jonah caught the plane back home. He couldn't wait to tell Ruby about the race.

Sophia excelled herself. She traced the Magrioni family tree right back to Venice, with Ruby's help, of course.

THE PLAGUE

1576

VENICE

Fifteen

Bruno Magrioni was a wealthy silk merchant in Venice, importing silk down the Silk Road from China. He lived in some style in a large house in Ruga dei Spezieri with his wife, Mary and his three children: Joseph, Ali and Ronata.

In 1570, Venice was the place to live. It was one of the richest countries in the world, built on trade. Henry Ford is often credited with inventing mass production on a production line. In fact, the Venetians beat him by 400 years. They were mass producing ships at The Arsenal in the 16th century. They had the biggest merchant fleet in the world at the time.

The plague changed everything.

When Ronata, his beautiful, blond 3 year old daughter, died of the plague, Bruno knew that he must move his family out of Venice or they would all die. He had seen the writing on the wall 6 months ago and began converting his wealth into gold and precious stones. The Ducat Venetian currency was in free fall, worth less with every passing day but it was taking time, too much time.

His faithful Chief Clerk, Costas Angram accompanied him on frequent visits to the mainland buying gold and jewellery. It was a hazardous occupation. They were in danger of being robbed at any time. He deposited the gold and jewellery in a safety deposit box at the Vatican Bank. He didn't even try selling his house, no one wanted property in Venice. He invited a couple of dealers to give him a price on the contents of his house, but the valuations were so derisory he threw the dealers out.

Before he left Venice, Bruno had to make his will, but the future could not have been more uncertain. No one knew if they would still be alive next week, let alone next year. In Venetian families, inheritance normally went down the male line. Bruno's son, Joseph could expect to inherit, but what if something happened to Joseph. He would have to make a will, but Joseph was only 8 years old. Who on earth was he going to leave his money to?

For three days and nights, Bruno wrestled with his will problem, trying to find a form of words that would cover every eventuality. He was worried that if something happened to him and Joseph, his wife and daughter would be left with nothing. In the end, his solicitor Mr Zaporetti came up with a form of words that was not unlike when you died intestate. Your relatives inherited your estate. Only, when you died intestate, a Judge decided who would inherit. In this case, Bruno was writing down in his will that all his relatives would inherit his estate, provided they could prove to his solicitor that they were his descendants. His solicitor would execute his will.

Antonia Angram, Costas Angram's wife, would not leave Venice. She had a large family there and she refused to abandon them and flee Venice with Bruno. So Bruno gave Costas, who was not only his Chief Clerk, but his right hand man, ten thousand pounds in gold, worth about £10 million today and free use of the ground floor of his house. Bruno told Costas to convert the ground floor to a shop, which was to be called Magrioni Maurano. In return, Costas and his descendants were to keep the rest of the house locked up secure until such times that a person or persons could prove to the Angram family that they were a descendant of him, Bruno Magrioni. If they were satisfied with the proof, they were to show Bruno's relatives the house.

Bruno and Costas signed a legal agreement to this effect. Costas would keep an eye on things in

Bruno's absence and let him know of any developments.

Bruno told his wife, Mary, to dress the children in rags and to find suitable scruffy clothes for themselves. He told her she could not take anything with her, only the clothes that they stood up in. They must have the appearance of desperate, poor people fleeing for their lives, which of course they were.

Bruno, Mary and their two surviving children climbed into their boat and set out across the Venetian Lagoon. Bruno kept a coach and horses on the mainland. The family climbed on board with Bruno at the reins.

As Bruno expected, they had only been travelling on their journey down the coast for a couple of days when they were stopped by highway robbers.

HIGHWAYMAN: 'Stop if you want to live!'

The Highwayman pointed his pistol at Bruno. There were four men altogether.

BRUNO: 'Stay back, sir. I have the plague and so has my wife. Mercifully, the children have not yet succumbed. We must get them somewhere that is clear of this dreadful disease if they are to survive.'

Mary had used make up to give herself and Bruno the appearance of having the plague. She knew all too well what it looked like.

The highwaymen pulled up their scarves that covered their nose and mouth.

HIGHWAYMAN: 'Throw out everything that you have got onto the road.'

BRUNO: 'Sir, we have nothing. Only the rags that we stand up in. We are fleeing from Venice. The city is like hell on earth. Everywhere there is death.'

The highwaymen looked at them, took in their scruffy appearance, and the lack of luggage on top of the coach. The four men talked to each other.

HIGHWAYMAN: 'That's a fine coach you have there.'

Bruno smiled. It was not a pleasant smile.

BRUNO: 'We are borrowing it. Let's just say the gentleman it belongs to won't be needing it anymore.'

They ordered Mary and the children out of the coach and the highwayman climbed inside. There was nothing there. He tried to lift the seat, first one side then the other. It wouldn't budge. The seat had a secret fixing device. If you didn't know the secret, you couldn't open it, which was just as well. Under the seat was a trunk which contained a considerable amount of gold.

Bruno was stood with his family watching the highwaymen.

BRUNO: 'That's the first thing I tried myself, it won't budge.'

The highwaymen climbed down from the coach. Young Joseph, who was about eight made a gun with his fist, pointed it at the Highwayman and said: 'Bang, bang. You're dead.'

Amazingly, they all laughed at that.

HIGHWAYMAN: 'He reminds me of my son. Go on, away with you. I will find somebody else to rob.'

They all climbed aboard the coach and set off. Joseph leaned out of the window and waved. The highwaymen waved back; unbelievably.

That wasn't the end of their ordeal, unfortunately. They were stopped again by highwaymen. In his childish way, Joseph told the men that he had already met a Highwayman and shot him: 'bang bang'. They laughed at the boy.

Bruno described the Highwayman. They knew who he was. If Julius had stopped them, he would have taken anything that was worth taking. There would be nothing left for them. It had happened before. They were going to have to do something about Julius.

They waved the coach on. Joseph was a star. Mary hugged him and kissed his head.

JOSEPH: 'What's that for?'

MARY: 'You are a brave boy, Joseph, standing up to those men.'

JOSEPH: 'I didn't like them, they had bad teeth.'

The signpost said 'PISA 5 miles'. They were passing through countryside, along the coast road. To the left was a farm, wheat fields, a vineyard, olive groves, fields with cattle and sheep in. 'It is very pleasant', thought Bruno. 'I like it here. The air is good, it smells fresh.' He stopped the horses and climbed down to the road.

BRUNO: 'Have a look, Mary, children. I like it here. What do you think?'

They all climbed down from the coach and looked around.

MARY: 'It's a nice place, Bruno. So different from Venice.'

JOSEPH: 'Can we go in the sea?'

ALI: 'Go in the sea!'

She was only five. She always copied what her brother said.

Bruno and Mary laughed, the first time they had done so in a very long time.

They drove into Pisa Town and Bruno turned into the stables of a coaching inn called the Pisa Hotel. He told them to sit tight while he went to see the Landlord.

Bruno walked into the bar. It was mid-afternoon and the place was deserted. He shouted: 'Landlord!' A big man with hands like hams and sweat standing out from his forehead, climbed up from the cellar below.

BRUNO: 'I am looking for two rooms for myself and my family. Can you accommodate us?'

The Landlord looked him up and down. He wasn't impressed with what he saw.

LANDLORD: 'And what makes you think you can afford such accommodation?'

Bruno took two gold coins out of his pocket and placed them on the bar. He left his fingers resting on the coins. The Landlord's eyes opened wide. He was looking at a month's rent at least.

BRUNO: 'Do not be fooled by my appearance, Sir. There is a reason for that which I will relate to you in the fulness of time. I am a silk merchant from Venice. I don't know if you know but Venice is not a good place to be right now.'

LANDLORD: 'I hadn't heard, Sir. Forgive me. I will send my boy to fetch your things and show you your rooms.'

BRUNO: 'We have no things Sir, just the clothes we are stood up in. There is my wife and two young children. We are tired and need to rest right now. I trust you can fix us up with a good meal later on.'

LANDLORD: 'Certainly, Sir. Do you have a preference?'

BRUNO: 'So long as it is good and hearty, that will be fine, my friend. We have been travelling for a week with little to eat and drink. You have not had a more appreciative customer.'

LANDLORD: 'Very good, Sir. If there is anything else I can help you with, I will be glad to oblige.'

Ruby Kind

BRUNO: 'There is something, but it will wait. We must rest first.'

Bruno, Mary, Joseph, and Ali collapsed into bed and slept solidly for four hours. When they eventually emerged, the Landlord's wife had set them a table in the back room.

She produced a large meat and potato pie, a bowl of carrots and another of green beans, plus a jug full of gravy. The Magrioni family fell on it like hungry wolves. The Landlord's wife, whose name was Loretta, beamed at their empty plates.

LORETTA: 'Now, that's what I like to see. Can anyone manage some apple pie?'

JOSEPH: 'Yes please!'

ALI: 'Yes please!'

They all laughed at the children.

BRUNO: 'I think they speak for all of us, thank you.'

When they had finished their meal, they took their drinks and sat by the fire. After a while, the Landlord and his wife: Aldo and Loretta, joined them. Bruno told them the tale of their flight from Venice.

ALDO: 'I had no idea it was so bad. I do know about Julius though, the Highwayman. He used to be a regular in here until he got caught stealing a cow. He took it to market and sold it – only it wasn't his to sell. It belonged to Count Mancini, as most things do round here. When the Count found out, he threw him off his land. He was lucky, most landlords would have had him arrested and thrown in jail. In view of what you have just said, that might have been the best thing to do.'

They all sat in silence for a while, each with their own thoughts, watching the fire.

BRUNO: We saw a very nice farm on our way in, about five miles distant. Wheat fields, a vineyard, an olive grove, sheep, and cattle. I am not a farmer myself, but it looked a very pleasant place to live. I've been wondering if it's a business that I might turn my hand to.'

ALDO: 'But that's Julius's farm Sir. The one who got thrown off his farm by Count Mancini. The Count is looking for someone to manage it.'

BRUNO: 'Would the Count consider selling it to me do you think?'

ALDO: 'He might at that. I heard a rumour that he is having money troubles. Something to do with his son. He always was a waster.'

BRUNO: 'What would be the best way to contact Count Mancini?'

ALDO: 'Through old Mr Heinrich Weismann, the solicitor. You'll find him in the Square, opposite the Tower. I wouldn't approach the Count direct, Sir. You are likely to get a frosty reception.'

Sixteen

Bruno was up early the following morning. He walked into town and bought a new jacket, breeches, shirt, and neckerchief. He took them back to the Inn and let his wife fuss over him. When she was satisfied with his appearance, she said he could go.

JOSEPH: 'When are we going to get new clothes, Dad?'

BRUNO: 'All in good time, son.'

MARY: 'Your father has an important meeting to go to, Joseph. He has to look his best.'

Bruno found the brass plate with *Heinrich Weismann, Solicitor* on it and knocked on the door. There was no reply. He knocked again. A woman passing by told him to come back at 10 o'clock: 'He will still be in bed,' she said. Rather than go back to the Hotel, Bruno wandered around the Leaning Tower of Pisa and the Cathedral or Duomo di Pisa. Good buildings, but not as good as Venice buildings. For the first time since their escape, Bruno was homesick. He wondered if he would ever see his home town again. The lean on the Tower didn't bother him, he liked quirkiness. Sometimes buildings can be too perfect. Before he became a silk merchant, Bruno was a builder; he built his own house.

At 10 past 10, he knocked again at the Solicitor's door. A small old gentleman with a few whisps of grey hair peaking out around his skull cap, answered the door.

BRUNO: 'Good morning, Sir. Sorry to disturb you. My name is Bruno Magrioni. I am interested in buying some property hereabouts. The Landlord of the Pisa Hotel where I am staying, Mr Aldo Mori advises me that you may be able to help me in this matter.'

MR WEISMANN: 'Yes, indeed, Sir. I am grateful to Mr Mori for recommending me. I must call in and see him. Come this way, Sir.'

The old solicitor led the way into a dusty room crammed with old books. A large desk sat in the middle of the room. Mr Weismann pulled out a chair for Bruno to sit on.

MR WEISMANN: 'Now then, Sir. Is there a particular property you are interested in?'

BRUNO: 'Yes. There is a farm, some five miles distant from Pisa on the coast road, which I believe has vacant tenancy. Mr Mori advises me that the property belongs to Count Mancini and that he may be interested in selling.'

MR WEISMANN: 'Mmm, he said that, did he? I wonder where he got that from. The Count has not expressed to me that he has any intention of selling.'

BRUNO: 'I believe there is a problem with his son.'

MR WEISMANN: 'I can well believe that. You must excuse me, Mr Magrioni. At my age I do not get out and about as much as I used to. I can see that certain events have failed to reach my ears. I will make an appointment to see the Count and discuss the matter with him. Will you be staying at the Pisa Hotel for a while?'

BRUNO: 'Yes, Sir. Until I find somewhere permanent to live.'

MR WEISMANN: 'Very well. I will contact you there.'

BRUNO: 'I do not wish to be impertinent, Mr Weismann, but you obviously act for the Count.

How can you obtain a good deal for me if you represent both parties?'

MR WEISMANN: 'You can be assured, Sir, that a fair and equitable price will be reached, taking into account the merits and demerits of both parties. You will not pay over the odds, Mr Magrioni. I can assure you of that. It is how we do things here.'

BRUNO: 'I am obliged to you, Sir. I did not mean to cause offence.'

MR WEISMANN: 'None taken, Sir. I'll bid you good day. There is much work to be done.'

Bruno walked back across the Square to the Pisa Hotel, shaking his head. Things were certainly done differently in the country, he thought. The lawyers would laugh about it in Venice.

Bruno met the Count in Mr Weismann's office. They both agreed the price that the old solicitor had arrived at and signed the deeds. There was no haggling. They all shook hands and that was that, the Magrionis had become farmers.

It was to be five years before Bruno returned to Venice. His Chief Clerk, Costas Angram, wrote to him occasionally. He told him the terrible disease seems to be abating. There was light at the end of the tunnel. Bruno was happy being a farmer in Pisa, but his profession was a silk merchant. He needed to know if he could return to Venice and resume his business.

In those days, women tended to be subservient to their husbands. They didn't challenge them. Mary said nothing when Bruno announced that he was going to pay a visit to Venice, but Bruno knew what she was thinking anyway. It was written all over her face.

BRUNO: 'Do not worry my love, I will be back within the week, I promise.'

Mary kissed him and held him tight. She had a terrific feeling of foreboding.

MARY: 'I shall not sleep a wink until you return.'

Bruno was in Venice less than a week when he caught the plague and died. No one knew why the plague killed some people quickly and allowed others to recover. The doctors had a theory that people who stayed in Venice developed a kind of resistance to the disease, whilst visitors who didn't have any resistance, succumbed to it quickly. Bruno had been away too long. Costas Angram, Bruno's Chief Clerk wrote to Mary with the sad news. She was devastated, so were the children. She couldn't even bring Bruno's body home to bury it, the Venice authorities wouldn't release it. They didn't want to spread the disease. Bruno was buried on the island of Lazzaretto Nuovo, along with other plague victims.

Two weeks later, Mary was reading in bed by the light of a candle. Since Bruno's death, she didn't sleep very well. It was a warm summer's night. She had the window open. Mary fell asleep in the early hours of the morning, exhausted. Her candle burnt on. A sudden wind rose up and rattled the bedroom window. It blew over the candle which landed on Mary's bed. Within a few minutes, the bedroom was a blazing inferno.

The children survived, but their mother did not. The farmhouse was a smouldering ruin. Joseph and Ali took refuge in one of the barns. It was a busy time at the farm. The wheat fields needed cutting, the cows always needed milking, and the grapes were ready for picking. They threw themselves into the work. There was no time to mourn. Mr Heinrich Weismann, the old solicitor, was very good. He organised the re-building of the farmhouse. He had access to Bruno's funds in Pisa. He did not, however, know about his estate in Venice. All Bruno's papers were combined in a large chest that sat at the foot of the matrimonial bed. In it were copies of the deeds for the Venice house, details of his safety deposit box at the Vatican Bank, papers relating to his silk merchant business, and a copy of his will.

All this was lost in the fire. The children didn't know that their father was worth a fortune. They worked hard on the farm, believing it to be their only income.

Costas Angram blamed himself for his boss's death. He should never have written to him telling him that Venice was getting better. He might just as well have put the noose around Bruno's neck.

Costas locked himself in his room and refused to come out. After three days, they broke down the door. Costas was dead. A little purple bottle was on his bedside table. The doctor smelled it: 'Arsenic', he said.

With Costas went Joseph and Ali's last link with their father's fortune, and so it remained. Amazingly, the Angram family remained true to the original agreement between Bruno Magrioni and Costas Angram and kept the house locked and secure, in return for use of the shop, rent free. Each generation passed on the story. There was something about the wording of that agreement and the circumstances of Bruno and Costa's deaths that no one dared contradict. Costas had left a full confession.

> *'I, Costas Angram, accept full responsibility for the death of my beloved employer, Bruno Magrioni. I cannot go on living with such a burden.'*
>
> *Costas Angram*

Joseph Magrioni died when he was 43, he and his sister Ali never married. They didn't have time for it. They just worked hard on the farm. They had each other, it was enough.

They had discussed what to do with the farm after they had gone and decided to give it to the church. They were both devout Catholics, but they hadn't got round to making a will.

After Joseph's funeral, Ali invited everyone round to the farmhouse for a wake. She invited as many people as she could think of: farmhands, neighbours, people from the town, the priest. She was on her own now Joseph had gone, she needed all the friends she could get. Already several people had said that if she needed help, she had only to ask.

They made their own wine at the farm, so there was plenty to drink. When it ran out, one of the farmhands went round to the barn and fetched some more. Everyone, including the priest, was getting steadily drunk. The wake went on into the night. No one wanted to be the first to leave. At some point during the evening, Ali fell asleep.

She woke up the following morning in her own bed, naked, with a naked man laying next to her. She couldn't remember a thing about the night before. The man was lying on his back with his mouth open, snoring. Ali lifted herself up on her elbow to see who it was. It was Leonardo, her stockman. She dropped back onto her pillow and stared at the ceiling. She wondered if anything had happened last night. She had never been in bed with a man before. She lifted up the bed clothes and looked. She reached out and touched him with the tip of her finger. Leonardo groaned and shifted his position. Ali quickly got out of bed. She didn't know if anything had happened last night, but if she wasn't careful, something could happen this morning.

She got dressed and went downstairs into the kitchen. She cut herself a slice of bread and poured some honey onto it. They made their own honey. She was sat at the kitchen table, slowly eating, trying to remember what had happened last night. She remembered talking to the priest. She told him that she was going to leave the farm to the church. He was very pleased and topped up her wine glass. And he kept topping up her wine glass.

Leonardo appeared at the kitchen door.

LEONARDO: 'What happened?'

ALI: 'Nothing, I hope. You had better get off home. Flavia and the kids, they will be worried. I'll milk the cows this morning. And try and get your story straight in your head, Leonardo, don't you dare mention me.'

LEONARDO: 'Thanks. I just want to say …'

ALI: 'Forget it, Leonardo, nothing happened. Go home to your wife.'

Leonardo walked across the yard and stopped. He had had an idea. He diverted to the barn and threw himself down on the straw. He rolled backwards and forwards, pulling the straw all over him. Straw stuck to his clothes and his hair.

LEONARDO: 'That should do. I woke up this morning in the barn. I don't remember anything about it. I just hope I can keep a straight face.'

Ali was sick a few times. She thought nothing of it, but after six months, there was no doubt. She had a definite bump. She was pregnant, She wondered if she should tell Leonardo but he noticed anyway. He had two children of his own. He knew what to look for.

ALI: 'Don't you dare leave Flavia and the kids. I'll manage. This is my problem, not yours.'

Flavia actually delivered Ali's baby. It's not so surprising really, she had helped out at several births in the town. She knew what to do. She was the obvious person to call. Flavia cut the umbilical cord and handed the baby to Ali. It was a boy. He was crying lustily.

FLAVIA: 'So, Ali, who is the father? There has been a great deal of speculation, but no one seems to know.'

ALI: 'I honestly don't know. It came as a complete surprise to me.'

FLAVIA: 'Ah, another immaculate conception. I've had one or two of those. There has to be a man, you know. I would have thought you, being a farmer, would know that.'

Flavia was smiling. Ali thought: 'If she knew the truth, she wouldn't be smiling.' From that moment on, Leonardo led a double life. Ali promoted him to Foreman and they ran the farm together. He spent as much time with Ali and baby Titus as he could. Titus never knew who his father was, but Leonardo treated him like a son. Ali daren't put Leonardo's name on Titus's birth certificate, so she left it blank.

Ali was 42 when Titus was born. 42 is old to be a mother nowadays, back then it was unheard of. The average life expectancy was 45. Ali lived to the grand old age of 55. Titus inherited the farm when he was 13. The whole Magrioni family is descended from him. If Ali hadn't had Titus, the farm would have gone to the church. The Magrioni family would have ended right there and Bruno's fortune would have been lost forever. It's amazing how a few bottles of wine can change the course of history.

Seventeen

Ruby and Paolo grew closer over the summer. It had started with Jonah and Ruby's first visit to Pisa. Ruby was stood by the back door of the farmhouse about 12 noon, watching Paolo work. It was a red hot summer's day, Paolo was stripped to the waist hoisting bales of hay up onto a haystack, the muscles of his lean, tanned body rippling as he stuck his pitchfork into each bale and hoisted it effortlessly into the air. Ruby didn't notice that Sophia had come up beside her.

SOPHIA: 'Handsome, isn't he!'

Ruby sighed.

RUBY: 'He's more than that. He's beautiful. I didn't know such a man existed in real life. I have only ever seen pictures of ancient statues that looked like that. He could be a Greek god!'

SOPHIA: 'He likes you too. He was asking me about you the other day. Why don't you take his lunch over to him. He'll be ready for that about now; he's been at it since 6 o'clock this morning. Take your own lunch and eat it with him in the barn.'

Ruby Kind

Ruby was learning Italian and Paolo was learning English. They sort of met in the middle. Back in York, Ruby sent Paolo e-mails and Paolo did his best to email back.

Sophia and Paolo were keen to see Jonah's farm in York. They caught the plane to Leeds Bradford airport and spent four days with them. It was all the time Paolo could afford. Ruby and Paolo hardly left each other's side.

It was the last week of the summer holidays for Ruby. Sophia had finally pieced together the last pieces of the Magrioni family tree and had invited Ruby and Jonah over to have a look. They walked into the dining room where Sophia had laid out the family tree on the big dining room table. She had drawn it on the back of a roll of wallpaper. A stack of certificates lay on the corner of the table: birth, marriage and death certificates, census forms, copies of church records, army records, newspaper cuttings and so on. The girls had worked hard. Sophia did all the leg work as everything was in Italian, but Ruby directed the search from her computer in York.

The Magrionis had lived in Pisa for a very long time. They tended to have small families, no more than one or two children, which was unusual in those days when families often comprised five or six children. The family did not originate in Pisa, however. Head of the family was Bruno Magrioni, his wife Mary and their three children: Joseph, Ali and Ronata. They came from Venice. Sophia had an address. They were going to have a look.

Jonah, Sophia, Paolo, and Ruby were stood in Ruga dei Spezieri, looking at a shop called *'Magrioni Maurano'*. It was on the ground floor of a substantial house, four stories high.

JONAH: 'Are you sure Bruno had no brothers or other relatives, Sophia?'

SOPHIA: 'I haven't found any.'

JONAH: 'Well, it looks like a branch of the family has been living in Venice all along if the sign on the shop is anything to go by.'

They looked in the window of the shop. It was filled with beautiful pieces of glassware: vases, jugs, animals.

RUBY: 'Can we go in and have a look?'

They all went into the shop. A young woman behind the counter was serving a couple of customers. When they had gone, Sophia went up to the woman.

SOPHIA: 'Good morning. I don't know if you can help us, but my name is Sophia Magrioni. This is my brother Paolo and these are my cousins, Ruby and Jonah, from England. We have traced our family tree right back to Bruno Magrioni, who used to live in this house.'

Sophia held up her father's old, leather, briefcase.

SOPHIA: 'I have a copy of the family tree and all the documents in here. Is the shop still in the hands of the Magrioni family? If so, we would very much like to meet them.'

The young woman had clapped a hand over her mouth and stared at Sophia with wide eyes.

The Angram family had waited for this moment for years. They never believed it would actually happen.

YOUNG WOMAN: 'I will ring my father, please wait here.'

She disappeared through the back. She returned after ten minutes.

YOUNG WOMAN: 'My father would like a word with you. Can you come through to telephone please.'

Sophia put the phone to her ear. A man on the other end said: 'My daughter tells me you have documents that prove you are related to Bruno Magrioni, is that right?'

SOPHIA: 'Yes, sir, that is right.'

YOUNG WOMAN'S FATHER: 'Would you mind showing them to my daughter and put her back on the phone.'

SOPHIA: 'Yes, of course.'

Sophia opened the briefcase and took out all the documents. The young woman looked at them and spoke to her father.

YOUNG WOMAN: 'Everything is here Dad, family tree, birth certificates, the lot. I think you should see it.'

The young woman handed the phone back to Sophia.

YOUNG WOMAN'S FATHER: 'I think we should meet. I will gather the other members of my family together. Can I suggest a meeting at 7 o'clock this evening?'

SOPHIA: 'Yes, of course.'

Ruby Kind

The young woman's father gave Sophia an address and said he looked forward to seeing them and having the opportunity to finally put right a wrong that had been done a very long time ago.

Jonah knocked on the door. Tobias Angram answered it. Tobias was the young shop woman's father that Sophia had talked to on the phone. He led them through to the dining room where eight people were sat round the table, waiting for them. Tobias made the introductions but Jonah was too excited to remember their names. The others said afterwards they were the same.

Sophia opened her briefcase and took out the roll of wallpaper that she had drawn the Magrioni family tree on. She unrolled it on the big table. The others held it down to stop it from curling up. Then she placed on the table the birth, marriage and death certificates and other papers. Starting with herself and Paolo on the farm at Pisa, she showed them the old photograph, taken before the war of four brothers: Luigi, Vincent, Giorgio, and Luca. Ruby pointed to each face and named them.

SOPHIA: 'Giorgio and Luca were killed in the war. Vincent stayed in England where he had been sent as a prisoner of war, leaving Luigi to run the farm at Pisa. Luigi is mine and Paolo's grandfather. He drowned along with my grandmother, my parents, and my maternal grandparents in a storm off the Greek island of Paros. They had all hired a boat for a holiday. It was something they had talked about doing for years. The boat sank. There were no survivors. Both sets of grandparents were recovered from the wreckage, but my parents have never been found.

The old man who sat next to Tobias sighed deeply and shook his head. This was Zagreb Angram, Tobias's father. He had thick white hair, piercing blue eyes, a ruddy complexion, and slightly purple lips. Sophia looked at him and thought 'blood pressure – I hope he doesn't have a heart attack.'

ZAGREB: 'Tragedy seems to follow our families. My wife was killed when a statue fell off the church at San Sebastiano and landed on top of her.'

Sophia translated for Ruby and Jonah. The conversation had been conducted in Italian. They all sympathised with Zagreb's loss.

Sophia took her time working through the Magrioni family tree, producing certificates and other papers. Finally, she got to Titus.

SOPHIA: 'As you can see, there is no father on Titus's birth certificate. His mother was called Ali Magrioni. I can't find a marriage certificate for Ali, but I have found a birth certificate. She was 42 when she had Titus, which is incredibly old to be having a baby in those days. It looks as though Titus was illegitimate. I have checked with a lawyer, and Titus is allowed to take his mother's name if no father is on his birth certificate. He is a true Magrioni, which is just as well, as everyone is descended from him.

Ali's father was Bruno Magrioni. He is listed as being a silk merchant in Venice. He had a wife, Mary and three children: Joseph, Ali and Ronata. They lived at Ruga dei Spezieri. That is all I know. I couldn't find a branch of the family still living in Venice. The first we knew of it was when we saw your shop, Magrioni Maurano.'

TOBIAS: 'We are not Magrionis. Our family name is Angram.'

ZAGREB: 'Tobias will explain, but I am satisfied that you are true descendants of Bruno Magrioni. I feel as though a huge burden has been lifted from my shoulders. The Angram family has carried the guilt of their ancestor, Costas Angram for hundreds of years. All we could do was honour the agreement between Bruno and Costas and hope that one day, Bruno's descendants would appear and we could open up the house. We dare not enter the house for fear it would bring bad luck on our family. Now you are here, I can die a happy man. I never thought this day would come.'

Sophia translated.

Sophia, Paolo, Ruby, and Jonah looked at each other, puzzled.

TOBIAS: 'I know you don't understand. I will explain.'

He spoke in English. Tobias placed an ancient-looking letter on the table.'

This is the agreement between your ancestor, Bruno Magrioni and my ancestor, Costas Angram. It reads:

'I, Bruno Magrioni, give my friend and trusted servant, Costas Angram, free use of the ground floor of my house in Ruga die Spezieri. It is to be used as a shop selling Maurano glassware. The shop is to be called Magrioni Maurano.

In return, the Angram family are to keep the rest of the house locked up and secure until such time as a person or persons can provide proof that they are descendants of me, Bruno Magrioni.

The house should then be opened and my descendants can take possession. They will find my will in the top right hand drawer of my desk.'

Sophia translated the letter for Ruby and Jonah.

TOBIAS: 'This is the agreement that we have stuck to all these years. The reason we have done this is because of this note.'

Tobias placed what looked like a hastily written note on paper that looked like it had been torn from a book. It read:

'I, Costas Angram, take full responsibility for the death of my beloved employer, Bruno Magrioni. I cannot live with this burden.

Signed:

COSTAS ANGRAM'

Again, Sophia translated.

JONAH: 'What does it mean: 'take full responsibility'?'

TOBIAS: 'We do not know. Family history records that Costas locked himself in his bedroom and refused to come out. Eventually, they knocked the door down and found him dead. He had taken arsenic. It was well known that there was much love between the two men. Costas was Bruno's Chief Clerk, but he was more than that. He was Bruno's right hand man. I don't think that Costas murdered Bruno; that would be unthinkable considering their relationship. So it must have been something else. Whatever it was, Costas obviously had a hand in it and could not live with himself.

This is the guilt that my father spoke of.'

Silence.

One of the children broke the spell.

YOUNG GIRL: 'Can we bring in the food now, Grandad? I'm starving.'

They all laughed at the youngster.

TOBIAS: 'Yes, of course, Brittany. We must celebrate. This is a great day. Tomorrow we will open up the house.'

Brittany's mother was a fan of Britney Spears when she was born and still was.

Eighteen

Zagreb, Jonah, Ruby, Sophia, and Paolo stood in the shop of Magrioni Maurano and watched Tobias put a large key into a large door. He turned it and pulled the handle. The door cracked and swung open to reveal a staircase. It was pitch black. Tobias snapped on a torch and led the way up the stairs. When he reached the top, it was still pitch black. He swung the torch around and noticed the shutters. He walked over to them and pulled them back. Light flooded into the room. They all gasped.

Ruby thought this must have been how Howard Carter felt when he entered the tomb of Tutankhamun. The large room that they were in was so lavishly furnished. Ruby didn't know where to look. Untouched by sunlight for centuries, the room was still the original, vibrant colours that it was first decorated in. They opened the rest of the shutters. It just got better. The landing was 10 foot wide, including the staircase. It ran the full width of the house. The long wall was lined with paintings and mirrors. The ceiling was painted with scenes from the Bible. The floor was covered in white, marble tiles. The stairwell wall was lined in red silk with oriental scenes picked out in gold. Along the long wall were console tables with ornately decorated pottery on them.

Ruby couldn't believe what she was looking at. She thought it was a painting of Mary and baby Jesus. There was only one person that she knew of that could paint this way: Leonardo da Vinci. If she was right, what would the painting be worth?

Paolo was calling them over. He thought he had found Bruno's office. They all walked into an oak panelled room with pictures of sailing ships hung on the walls. In the middle of the room was a large desk.

PAOLO: 'The drawers are locked. Can you try your keys, Tobias?'

Tobias had a large keyring full of keys. He selected a key and tried it. It wouldn't turn. He tried another and another. Finally, he found one that fitted and pulled open the drawer. Inside was a metal box, about a foot long, 3 inches wide, and 3 inches deep. Tobias pulled it out. It was very heavy.

JONAH: 'Is it bronze?'

TOBIAS: 'I think so.'

Ruby Kind

Around the edge of the box, was a lot of little keys, like piano keys. They were ivory with black letters on them. Each key had a letter of the alphabet. They all peered at the strange box, trying to work out what it was.

SOPHIA: 'There's a piece of paper in the drawer, Tobias.'

Tobias picked up the piece of paper and unfolded it.

TOBIAS: 'It's in Bruno's handwriting, but he hasn't signed it. It says:

> *'Press down the keys that correspond to the first letter of my name, my wife's name and my children's names.'*

TOBIAS: 'Do you know the names, Sophia?'

Sophia was smiling: 'I certainly do.'

She opened her briefcase, took out the roll of wallpaper and unfurled it on Bruno's desk. She ran her finger up to the top of the family tree and read out the names:

'B for Bruno, M for Mary, J for Joseph, A for Ali, and R for Ronata.'

As Sophia read out each letter, Tobias pressed the keys on the metal box. They stayed down. When he pressed the last one, they all heard the click. Tobias opened the lid of the box. Inside was a scroll. He took the scroll out and handed it to Jonah.

TOBIAS: 'As head of the Magrioni family, I think you should open it, Jonah.'

Jonah hadn't thought of himself as being head of the Magrioni family, but as eldest, he supposed he must be. The scroll was sealed with a red, wax seal. In the centre of the seal was the initials 'BM'. Jonah used his thumb nail to prise open the seal. He unfurled the scroll and handed it to Sophia. He couldn't read it. Sophia translated.

SOPHIA: 'The wording is similar to the agreement between Costas Angram and Bruno. It must have been written at the same time. It says:

> *'I, Bruno Magrioni, leave my entire estate to any person or persons that can prove that they are related to me. This proof is to be presented to my solicitor, Mr Zaporetti, who will execute this will.*
>
> *My estate comprises the house on Ruga die Spezieri and its contents, plus the contents of my safety deposit box at the Vatican Bank.'*

Jonah turned to Sophia.

JONAH: 'If you hadn't have known those names, we would never have been able to open this box and we would never have known that Bruno had left his estate to us.'

SOPHIA: 'I think that was what Bruno intended. He thought one of his children would open the box. No one else would know about Ronata, but thanks to the internet, we have been able to find her birth certificate and death certificate. He could never have imagined that it would be all those years later until it was opened.'

JONAH: 'What do we do now?'

RUBY: 'We try and find Bruno's solicitors. I very much doubt that they will still be there, but they may have left a paper trail for us to follow.'

Paolo led the way. He had bought a map of Venice and had decided that the best way to get where they wanted to be was by gondola.

Tobias and Zagreb stayed behind at the house. The will was none of their business. They had fulfilled their obligations to Bruno Magrioni. A black cloud had been lifted from the Angram family. They just wanted to look around the house that they had been custodians of for so many years.

Paolo, Sophia, Jonah, and Ruby boarded a gondola on the Grand Canal.

They found the street easily enough, but it had obviously changed out of recognition since Bruno's days. It was mostly shops now. What they needed was a house number, but the shops didn't have any numbers, they just had names.

Paolo, Sophia, and Ruby split up and walked into some of the shops to try and find out their street numbers. There was no point in Jonah going into the shops. He wouldn't have understood a word they said. So he just wandered about.

It started to rain. Jonah slipped into a café to shelter. He sat down at one of the tables. After a while, a waitress came over to him and asked him if he was ready to order. She had spoken to him in English, with an Italian accent.

JONAH: 'How did you know I was English?'

The girl smiled; her name was Marie. She put her head on one side.

MARIE: 'I think it is the jumper and the haircut. No Italian man would have a jumper and haircut like that.'

They both laughed and introduced themselves.

JONAH: 'I'll have a cappuccino and a sticky bun, please, Marie, I'm not bothered which type.'

When Marie came back, Jonah decided to ask her the question.

JONAH: 'I'm looking for Zaporetti Solicitors. I don't suppose you know the street number of this café, do you?'

MARIE: 'I don't, but look on the wall behind you.'

Jonah looked. There was a brass plaque fixed on the wall that said *'Zaporetti Solicitors'*.

JONAH: 'Well I never! Are they still here?'

MARIE: 'Well, if they are, I've never seen them. That plaque has been there forever. I can ask my boss if you like.'

JONAH: 'That would be great. Thanks, Marie.'

Marie came back and placed a card on Jonah's table. It said:

'Zaporetti Solicitors
2 Strada Nova
Venice'

MARIE: 'My boss says he rents the café from them.'

JONAH: 'Thanks Marie. You're a star!'

Ruby was peering in the café window. She held a plastic bag on her head. It was raining. She spotted Jonah. Jonah waved and she came in. Sophia and Paolo followed. They were all a bit damp.

RUBY: 'It's alright for some! We've been working.'

They all sat down at Jonah's table.

JONAH: 'Fear not, my children. Uncle Jonah has solved the problem. Or should I say, my good friend Marie here has solved it.'

Jonah pushed the solicitor's card towards them.

Ruby picked up the card and looked at Marie.

RUBY: 'You know these people, Marie?'

MARIE: 'I don't, no. But my boss does. He rents the café from them.

RUBY: 'I don't understand. From the house numbers that we've been able to find out, the office should be down by the Grand Canal.'

JONAH: 'Maybe they moved.'

Nineteen

Sophia walked up to the receptionist at Zaporetti Solicitors and asked to see Mr Zaporetti.

RECEPTIONIST: 'I am afraid there are no Zaporettis in the firm any longer. We just keep the name. The Managing Partner is Mr Bellini.'

SOPHIA: 'Can we see him then?'

RECEPTIONIST: 'May I ask what it is about?'

SOPHIA: 'Yes. We have a very ancient will that was drawn up by Mr Zaporetti in 1576. We are the heirs and we would like a solicitor to execute the will.'

Ruby took Bruno's will out of the briefcase and laid it on the receptionist's desk.

RECEPTIONIST: 'I see.'

She tapped away at her computer.

RECEPTIONIST: 'Would next Wednesday at 10 o'clock suit you?'

RUBY: 'Is it possible to do it sooner? We have come all the way from York in England, or should I say me and my uncle Jonah have. Sophia and Paolo are from Pisa.'

RECEPTIONIST: 'Just a minute.'

She picked up her phone and spoke into it.

RECEPTIONIST: 'Mr Bellini will see you for five minutes. Please don't delay him. He's due in court in half an hour.'

Sophia introduced them all to Mr Bellini and showed him Bruno's will.

MR BELLINI: 'Interesting. You have the proof that you descended from Bruno Magrioni?'

SOPHIA: 'Yes, we do.'

She opened her briefcase and started to get out the documents.

MR BELLINI: 'No, no. I haven't got time for that now. Meet me at this office at 8 o'clock Saturday morning.'

SOPHIA: 'Thank you, Mr Bellini. We really appreciate that.'

Unexpectedly, the solicitor gave them a beaming smile.

MR BELLINI: 'I know of one other case like this. It is still proceeding. No figures have emerged yet, but there is great speculation at my club. Everyone is expecting it to be big. I am really looking forward to this.'

He hustled them out of his office.

This was Thursday morning. They had two days to wait. So they went back to Bruno's house and joined Tobias and Zagreb.

Sophia, Paolo, Jonah, and Ruby were fifteen minutes' early on Saturday morning at Zaporetti's office. Mr Bellini arrived bang on time. He led them up to his office and settled himself behind his desk.

MR BELLINI: 'Now then, young lady, let's have a look at this family tree of yours.'

Ruby laid it out on his desk and carefully went through it, producing the certificates to go with it.

MR BELLINI: 'Well, in a court of law, I think you have proved your claim, but there seems to be someone missing, err, Aileen Fish, nee Magrioni. That would be your mother, Ruby.'

RUBY: 'Yes, that's right. She hasn't taken any part in this. In fact, when I mentioned it to her, she didn't want to know.'

MR BELLINI: 'Curious. Still, I don't see that it matters. We can catch up with her later.'

Mr Bellini went to a filing cabinet, pulled out a drawer, and took out some forms. He gave them each one.

MR BELLINI: 'If you would just sign on the dotted line and print your name below.'

They all did that and handed back the forms.

MR BELLINI: 'Can you give that form to your mother, Ruby, and ask her to post it back to me.'

RUBY: 'I'll try.'

MR BELLINI: 'Are you sure there wasn't a key in the bronze box that you found Bruno's will in?

PAOLO: 'There was no key, only the scroll.'

MR BELLINI: 'We need a key to open the safety deposit box at the Vatican Bank. A letter of authority from the Bank would also be useful. These things are often signed by the Pope. In my experience, people don't put things in a safety deposit box at the Vatican Bank unless they have something very valuable that they want to keep safe.

It's the devil's own job to get anything out of the Vatican Bank. They take their role of custodian very seriously, which, I suppose, is what people want them to do when they give them their valuables to keep.

The only other place I can think that the key will be is with our copy of Bruno's will, which means we will have to search for it. Would you mind helping me search?'

SOPHIA: 'Yes, of course.'

Mr Bellini led the way to the café where Jonah had stumbled upon the Zaporetti Solicitors sign. He shook hands with the Manager and explained that they were going upstairs to look for some documents.

MR BELLINI: 'Any chance of some coffee?'

MANAGER: 'OK, but you will have to wait. As you can see, we're very busy.'

Mr Bellini opened one of the doors on the landing. It led into a room stacked floor to ceiling with files.

MR BELLINI: 'I suggest we split up and take a section each.'

Ruby soon realised that the files were in a complete mess. There was no order to them whatsoever. Files from the 1800s were next to files from the 1600s. People with names beginning with B were next to people with names beginning with N. They were going to have to look at every file. There could be no short cuts.

Marie came in with the coffees.

MARIE: 'I had no idea any of this was here.'

JONAH: 'If it wasn't for you, Marie, we might never have found this. You really must let us get you something.'

MARIE: 'I'll think about it.'

By lunchtime, they had looked at every file in the room, but to no avail. Mr Bellini took them downstairs to the café and bought them something to eat and drink. Ruby said what was on all of their minds.

RUBY: 'I thought solicitors were supposed to be organised, methodical. This place is a shambles.'

MR BELLINI: 'Ah, there is a reason for that, my dear. We used to have a magnificent office fronting onto the Grand Canal. During the Second World war, the Germans commandeered it for their headquarters. They gave us 24 hours to pack up and get out. The files were transported in handcarts during the middle of the night. This house happened to be empty, so we piled everything in here. If we hadn't, the Germans would have thrown them out into the street and set fire to them. I don't know this myself, of course, it is what my grandfather had told me.'

RUBY: 'I thought your office was down by the Canal. Weren't the Italians on the same side as the Germans during the war?'

MR BELLINI: 'Mussolini and his henchmen were. The Italian people hated the Germans. They greeted the British like heroes when they drove them out.

I know we should have done something about the files before now. We did actually employ a couple of students during their summer holidays to have a go at it. It doesn't look like they did much. Bear with me a while longer. We'll do another couple of hours then pack it up. I'll just have to approach the Vatican Bank with Bruno's will and hope that they will help me. I may have to make an appointment to see the Pope.'

They all trudged back upstairs and started on the next room. Ruby wondered about opening doors. She wanted to see how big a haystack they were looking in. In one of the rooms, files were piled in a great heap in the middle of the floor. One of the rooms was locked. She went back and asked Mr

Bellini if she could borrow his keys. So far he hadn't had to use them, all the doors had been open, apart from one at the bottom of the stairs.

Ruby tried a few keys before she found one that fitted. She opened the door.

RUBY: 'Ah, now this is better.'

The files were neatly arranged on the shelves. They didn't quite reach the ceiling. At the beginning of each row was a card with a date on it. Along the rows were letters of the alphabet. Ruby ran her finger round until she found 16th century, selected the letter M and started pulling out files.

RUBY: 'Bingo!'

She walked into the room where the others were searching and placed an ancient box file on the table.

RUBY: 'I don't know how much you paid those students, Mr Bellini, but whatever it was it was not enough. They have done a grand job. You should get them back.'

She pointed to the box file.

RUBY: 'Magrioni.'

MR BELLINI: 'Where did you get that?'

RUBY: 'From the locked room. You should see it. It's like a library.'

They all sat round the table and Mr Bellini sifted out papers carefully from the file, one by one. The top four sheets referred to Bruno's silk merchant business.

MR BELLINI: 'Ah, here we are.'

He lifted out Bruno's will. Underneath was a letter from the Pope. It read:

> *'I, Pope Gregory XIII, give legal authority to Bruno Magrioni and family to open Box 9 and dispose of the contents therein.*
>
> *Signature of Pope Gregory XIII'*

MR BELLINI: 'Excellent.'

He carefully lifted out the letter. Underneath was an elaborate bronze key. The handle of the key was a pierced metal design. In the centre was engraved the number 9. Wound around the barrel of the key was a snake. Not a real one, an engraved snake.

MR BELLINI: 'Well, that looks genuine enough, doesn't it. Well done Ruby.'

ALL: 'Well done Ruby.'

Ruby did her impression of the Queen waving from the balcony.

RUBY: 'Thank you, plebs. Grovel.'

They all laughed at that.

Downstairs, they bumped into Marie.

JONAH: 'We found what we wanted, Marie!'

MARIE: 'That's great! You'll be wanting to celebrate then?'

JONAH: 'I suppose we should celebrate, yes. What do you think, guys?'

RUBY: 'Good idea. Any idea where?'

MARIE: 'There's a new place opened up on Campo San Barnaba called Alexandria's. That's supposed to be good. I can book us a table if you like.'

JONAH: 'You'll come?'

MARIE: 'Just try and stop me.'

Ruby, Jonah, Sophia Paolo, Tobias, Zagreb, Marie, Mr Bellini and his wife were all sat round a large table in Alexandria's Restaurant. They had had their main course and were waiting for their sweet. Marie had been right. The food was good. Mr Bellini tapped his wine glass with his pen and cleared his throat.

MR BELLINI: 'I would like to propose a toast to the Magrioni family who have risen like a Phoenix from the ashes. The Magrioni family.'

ALL: 'The Magrioni family.'

The sweets came, more wine was ordered. Jonah had made a pass at Marie. She didn't seem to mind. They were holding hands underneath the table.

Twenty

Ruby got straight As in her Music, Art, and History GCSEs. Her other 5 GCSEs she passed at lesser grades. She moved into the sixth form to study A levels in those subjects. The rest of her band, Ruby Kind, did the same.

Ruby Kind had played steadily over the summer holidays. They were developing a following in York. They were getting paid – so much so, the taxman was taking an interest. They all got a shock when they received a demand from the Inland Revenue.

A levels were a two year course. Ruby had already completed the first year last term. In an attempt to keep her interested and stop her from playing truant, her teachers had given her extra work. She devoured it like a hungry animal. She didn't need to work hard. She found it easy. I have come across people like that when I did my own A levels. I used to call them geniuses. They would help the teacher out if he got stuck on anything. I wasn't a genius; in fact I was at the bottom of the class. But that was just because I was studying the wrong subjects.

Ruby Kind

Ruby sat at the back of the class and started on the second year of the A level syllabus whilst the rest of the class started on the first.

Ruby's teachers held a meeting in the staff room. Ruby had completed the A level courses in Music, Art, and History. They were discussing what to do with her.

MISS EYEBALL: 'The obvious thing to do is to enter her for the exams this year, a year early. I have no doubt she would pass at an A grade.'

MR SMALES: 'I agree, we need to see the Headmaster.'

MR CRABTREE: 'I have never known anyone like her. She just soaks history up like a sponge. She knows more than me about the Second World War.'

MISS EYEBALL: 'That's agreed then. I'll make an appointment to see the headmaster.'

ALL: 'Yes.'

Ruby was not Mr Cuticle's favourite pupil. Mr Cuticle was the Headmaster. He still hadn't forgiven her for playing truant last year. She had got him into trouble with the Chief School Inspector. He had never been in trouble with a School Inspector in his life before. It still smarted when he thought about it. When the three teachers asked him to enter Ruby for her A levels a year early, he scowled at them.

MR CUTICLE: 'And what makes you think she is capable of taking these exams?'

The three teachers were ready for this question. They all had Ruby's marks for the last year. She hadn't been below 90%.

MR CUTICLE: Mmm, she can do it, if she wants to then … I really don't see why I should put myself out for the likes of Ruby Fish. She doesn't deserve it.'

MISS EYEBALL: 'She only played truant because she was bored. Keep her interested and she is brilliant.'

MR CUTICLE: Hmmph. I'll think about it, but I'm not promising anything.'

The three teachers left the Headmaster's office. Mr Cuticle had no intention of doing anything for Ruby Fish.

So Ruby entered the final year of the A level course with nothing to do. Her teachers raided their attics and brought down their University notes. They set

Ruby projects to do based on their University courses. To do these projects, Ruby had to use the library both at the school and in the town. She did most of her work in the libraries. She was careful to do these projects diligently. She enjoyed her new-found freedom and didn't want to give her teachers any reason for not trusting her. She seldom attended class, but her teachers marked her down as 'present' anyway.

Ruby, being Ruby, however, she could not resist a bit of fun when it was presented to her. Ruby was a part time life model at York's two universities.

Mr Smales, the Art teacher, had engaged a life model. When he told the class about it, they were all excited, looking forward to it, especially the boys. It was to be a female life model.

Ruby watched this grey haired, old woman make her way to the front of the Art class. She was wearing a white towelling bathrobe. Mr Smales introduced her to the class as Agnes.

AGNES: 'Good morning boys and girls. You were probably hoping for an Elle Macpherson look-alike, but all you've got is little old me. Try not to be too disappointed. It will be good practice for you, drawing all my wrinkles.'

The class laughed, but the boys did look disappointed. Agnes took off her bathrobe. She was wearing white knickers and a white bra underneath. Ruby waited for her to take them off, but she didn't. She just sat down on a chair that Mr Smales had placed in front of the class and composed herself.

The class started to draw. Mr Smales walked around giving guidance to his pupils. He saved Ruby till last. It was nearly packing up time when he got to her.

MR SMALES: 'Come and have a look at this, Agnes.'

Agnes got up from her chair and came over.

AGNES: 'Very good, dear. You could give them a run for their money at the University. Pity I wasn't naked.

RUBY: 'Why weren't you naked, Agnes?'

MR SMALES: 'The headmaster wouldn't allow it.'

AGNES: 'Stupid old prude. What he needs is a night with a mucky woman. I could teach him a thing or two.'

They both laughed at the thought of Mr Cuticle with a mucky woman.

AGNES: 'If you would like to paint me naked, dear, you could always come to my flat. There is only me and the budgie.'

RUBY: 'Would that be alright, Sir?'

MR SMALES: 'It's your time, Ruby. You can do what you like. It would help your portfolio if you drew and painted a nude, I must admit.'

Mr Smales walked back to the front and dismissed the class.

RUBY: 'Can I buy you a drink, Agnes?'

It was lunchtime.

AGNES: 'I wouldn't say no to a G and T.'

Ruby and Agnes were sat in the pub.

RUBY: 'Do you mind if I ask how old you are, Agnes?'

AGNES: 'Not at all. I'm 62.'

RUBY: 'You've got an amazing body for someone of 62.'

AGNES: 'You have to keep yourself in good shape in this business. It's my livelihood. Having said that,

I would like to retire, but they can't find a replacement that will do it for the money they pay.'

RUBY: 'Who is 'they'?'

AGNES: 'The two Universities: York and St John. I don't normally do schools. I only did it as a favour to Eddie. I've known him since he was a student.'

RUBY: 'Who is Eddie?'

AGNES: 'Eddie Smales.'

RUBY: 'Oh. I didn't know his Christian name.'

AGNES: 'Would you like to come to my flat and draw me?'

RUBY: 'I would, but I'm afraid I wouldn't be able to pay you much either.'

AGNES: 'Oh don't worry about that. I'll be glad of the company. Shall we say 7.30 tomorrow night?'

RUBY: 'Great. I'll look forward to that. Thanks Agnes.'

Ruby and Agnes got on like a house on fire. After a couple of visits, Ruby said what was on her mind.

RUBY: 'Do you think I could take over from you as a life model, Agnes?'

Ruby Kind

AGNES: 'I don't see why not. You look like you've got a good body. Take your clothes off, let's have a look.'

Ruby was a big girl: 5 foot 10 with a well-developed, curvaceous figure, for her age. She had thick, blond, shoulder-length hair parted in the middle and lively, intelligent, blue eyes. I suppose her face was quite plain, until she smiled. She had a knockout smile. If you hadn't seen it before, you tended to stare. She had learned to use this smile. It generally got her what she wanted, but she was careful not to wear it out.

Ruby took her clothes off. Agnes walked round, examining her carefully.

AGNES: 'Mmm, do you exercise?'

RUBY: 'I play hockey.'

AGNES: 'You need to lose about 6 or 7 pounds. Exercise more, eat the right things. I can give you some recipes. You should be fine.'

RUBY: 'Do you think they'll like me?'

AGNES: 'They'll wet themselves, love. They won't be able to believe their luck.'

Ruby smiled.

AGNES: 'How old are you, Ruby?'

RUBY: 'I'm seventeen.'

AGNES: 'It's old enough. I was fifteen when I started stripping.'

RUBY: 'My Gran was a stripper during the war. She worked at the Windmill Theatre in London.'

AGNES: 'Did she now? I've heard of the Windmill. Well, well, well. So you could say taking your clothes off runs in the family.'

RUBY: 'I guess it does.'

AGNES: 'Are you serious about this, Ruby?'

RUBY: 'Certainly am.'

AGNES: 'Great! I can retire. I'll organise a party and you can meet the lecturers from the Universities that hire me. Use that smile of yours and they'll be bowled over.'

———————————

Ruby was a bit nervous at first, sat in front of a group of students, naked, but as her Gran had said: 'You got used to it'. It didn't bother her now. A few of the students had tried chatting her up, but she didn't go out with any of them. Agnes had warned her against that. It got complicated when you broke up. It could even lose her the job.

Whilst she was at the University, Ruby made use of the library. The lecturers had a card made up for her so that she could use the library as a student. It gave her a legitimate reason for being at the University if anyone asked.

Twenty-one

Ade Montgolfier still sang occasionally in the folk clubs. Ruby Kind tended to play at the weekends. Ade was a regular on Thursday nights at the Folk Club at the Black Duck on Peasholme Green, so it didn't clash. He had invited the band to the Folk Club to see Noah Moore. He wouldn't elaborate. He said he wanted it to be a surprise, but he said they were in for a treat. Ruby was intrigued. She had heard Ade sing at the Folk Club before which was how she came to choose him for Ruby Kind, but there was something about this Noah Moore that Ade wasn't telling them.

Ade had finished his turn. The audience were clapping as the landlord made his way to the microphone.

LANDLORD: 'Thanks Ade. Good as ever. Now we've got a rare treat for you, back by popular demand, at great expense, all the way from the Emerald Isle, the one and only Noah Moore.'

Huge applause greeted a huge man as he made his way to the stage. He must have been at least 6 foot 7 inches and built like a tank. He had a mass of ginger hair and a huge ginger beard. Slung round his neck was a banjo. It was a normal sized instrument but on him it looked like a toy. In his right hand he held a large glass half full with Guiness. Ruby asked Ade what it was. He said it was a 'quart pot': two pints. The Landlord kept it specially for Noah. He was the only one who could handle it.

Noah wasn't on his own. He had a band. They were all completely different. There was a youth with long, blond hair that played a guitar; a little old, man with a shiny bald head that played a fiddle; and an amazing looking girl with long, jet black hair, a very pale – almost ghostly – white complexion, ruby red lips, she wore no make-up, green eyes and she wore a green dress, embroidered with Celtic designs. This was Caitlin. Ade had seen her before, he had tried talking to her, but she had such a strong Irish accent he couldn't understand a word she said. He was content to watch, for now. Caitlin played a hand drum called a bodhran. She also danced an Irish jig, in her black leather clogs.

Noah bellowed into the microphone.

NOAH: 'NOW THEN ENGLISH, HOW YA DOIN?'

The audience laughed and clapped.

NOAH: 'Arr, get some Guiness down your neck, you'll be fine. LANDLORD, THERE'S A MAN HERE WITH NO PINT IN HIS HAND, SHAKE YOURSELF!'

The Landlord scuttled over and thrust a pint of Guiness into the man's hand. Noah fiddled about tuning his banjo.

NOAH: 'I suppose we'll have to play you something.'

LANDLORD: 'That's what I'm paying you for.'

The audience laughed and jeered.

NOAH: 'Arr, he's not a bad man, for an English. We'll start with '*Whisky in the Jar*', boys. Just a minute.'

The big man drained his glass and held the quart pot at arm's length.

NOAH: 'Landlord! Fill her up.'

Free beer was included in Noah's fee.

A girl sat on the front row, stood up and took the glass. She passed it to the row behind who did the same. When it reached the back, a man stood up and placed the glass on the bar. The Landlord filled it with Guiness and waited for it to settle. When it was ready, he nodded to the man at the back who collected it and passed it to the row in front. When it reached the front, the girl placed it on the stage. Noah was in mid-song, but he still managed to give the girl a lecherous leer and an outrageous wink. The girl blushed to her roots. It all looked impromptu, but it was actually well rehearsed, except for the blush, that was genuine enough. When they rehearsed it last night, they hadn't told the girl what to expect from Noah. Now she knew why. She was the only one that volunteered. Noah was every mother's nightmare.

It was a classic folk song. Everyone knew the words and sang along.

WHISKEY IN THE JAR

Whack fall the daddy-o,
whack fall the daddy-o
There's whiskey in the jar

Noah followed it with another classic:

WILD ROVER

I've been a wild rover for many a year
And I've spent all my money on whiskey and beer
I asked her for credit, she answered me: nay
Now I never will play the wild rover no more

Paul Philip Studer

*And it's no, nay, never
No, nay, never, no more
And I'll play the wild rover
No never, no more.*

Everyone sang along again.

NOAH: 'You won't know this next song. It was written by a friend of mine from Donegal. He says it's a true story, but the truth gets a bit blurred in Ireland on account of the drink. I'll have to teach you the chorus. PAY ATTENTION!'

The audience jumped. Noah roared with laughter.

NOAH: 'That made you jump.'

Noah was pointing to someone in the audience.

NOAH: 'Right, listen up, as our American cousins say. Here's the chorus.'

*Come alive with me Bonny Beaty
Come alive with me in Donegal
Come alive with me when they've all gone out to sea
Bonny Beaty you're the prettiest of them all*

'OK, got that? Off you go'

The audience made a ragged attempt at the chorus.

NOAH: 'What a shambles! I'll have to sing it meself. Diamond, play us in will you?'

Diamond was the bald fiddle player.

BONNY BEATY

Come alive with me Bonny Beaty
Come alive with me in Donegal
Come alive with me when they've all gone out to sea
Bonny Beaty you're the prettiest of them all

She was only seventeen, a young and innocent Colleen
When I kissed her down O'Mally's Country Fair
Well she coloured up bright red, and said:
'Sir, if you are wed
You'd be better off instead with your Potcheen'

Come alive with me Bonny Beaty
Come alive with me in Donegal
Come alive with me when they've all gone out to sea
Bonny Beaty you're the prettiest of them all

Well the sun was far too strong and we lingered far too long
I saw a longing look just creep into her eye
We made love in the hay stack neath an oak beam,
on a sack
And now that's the end of that, I'll tell you no more

She come alive with me Bonny Beaty
Come alive with me in Donegal
Come alive with me when they've all gone out to sea
Bonny Beaty you're the prettiest of them all

*Now we're wed and that's alright and we've started a new life
But we still go walking down in Donegal
I get pleasure every night, it's such a beautiful new sight
To see her smiling with the baby in her arms*

*Come alive with me Bonny Beaty
Come alive with me in Donegal
Come alive with me when they've all gone out to sea
Bonny Beaty you're the prettiest of them all
Bonny Beaty you're the prettiest of them all
Bonny Beaty you're the prettiest of them all*

By the end of the song, the audience had got the hang of the chorus. They would know it next time. Ade liked the song; he might use it himself. He would try and have a word with Davey about it after the gig. Davey was the long haired youth playing the guitar. It would be no use talking to Noah. By that time he would be so pissed he wouldn't remember anything.

Noah followed this song with another favourite: '*You're drunk, you're drunk, you silly old fool*'. Like a lot of his songs, it featured the demon drink.

*You're drunk, you're drunk, you silly old fool
Still you cannot see,
that's a baby boy that me mother sent to me*

Ruby Kind

Well it's many a road I've travelled, a hundred miles or more
But whiskers on a baby boy, I've never seen before

They all had a good night. Ruby could see why Ade didn't want to give it up.

Twenty-two

Ruby's friend, Veronica, had given Ruby and her mother and father complimentary tickets for a ballet that she was appearing in at the Theatre Royal. When they were little girls, Ruby and Veronica had attended ballet lessons together. It was Veronica's mum's idea. She used to be a ballerina, but had given it up to have a family. She had a secret ambition for her daughter. She wanted her to be a prima ballerina, something she had never managed herself, but she told no one about it, not even Veronica. She didn't want to put her under pressure. Veronica's mother encouraged and helped her, but she never pushed.

Aileen had no such ambition, but there was a certain kudos to having a daughter in ballet school. She liked talking about it, bragging. But Ruby grew tall, taller than the boys. They couldn't lift her. One day the Principal took her to one side and suggested that she tried something else.

Veronica, though, carried on. She was petite. She was good. She starred in many of the school's productions. When she was sixteen, the principal

Ruby Kind

got her into the Northern Ballet, after she had taken her GCSEs.

The Northern Ballet were performing tonight. Veronica had a starring part. She was performing a new ballet called 'Dreaming' with a young Russian ballet dancer called Vladimir.

Ruby, Aileen, Maurice and Veronica's Mum and Dad, Lola and Zack were sat in the auditorium waiting for the curtain to go up. Ruby couldn't remember the last time she had been out with her parents. It was a long time ago and she hadn't seen Veronica's parents for years, but she still wanted to go. She wanted to see Veronica in her element. She wanted to see her dance. Ruby had been disappointed when the Principal had told her to leave the ballet school. She enjoyed dancing, but she was right, of course. She could quite easily have lifted most of the boys herself.

There was another reason that Ruby wanted to go to the Theatre: Veronica had written to her and invited her to the after-show party. She wanted to introduce her to her new boyfriend: Vladimir Vorodin. Vladimir was playing Veronica's boyfriend in the ballet.

The curtain went up revealing a backdrop of a beautiful, sunlit, wild flower meadow: long grass, blue, yellow, pink, white flowers and over to the right was a young girl, sleeping.

Veronica and Vladimir ran onto the stage from opposite wings. They met in the middle, embraced, and began to dance. Part way through, Vladimir gave Veronica a single, blue cornflour. She held it to her nose, then placed it in her hair. Seamless, beautifully done.

DREAMING

Young girl sleeping in the long grass mmmm
Young girl sleeping in the long grass mmmm
Young girl sleeping in the long grass mmmm
Young girl sleeping in the long grass mmmm

Young girl sleeping in the long grass mmmm
Young girl sleeping in the long grass mmmm
Young girl sleeping in the long grass mmmm
Young girl sleeping in the long grass mmmm

Dreaming of her sweet companion
Dreaming of her sweet young man
Oo oo oo

Dreaming of her sweet companion
Dreaming of her sweet young man
Oo oo oo
Oo oo oo
Oo oo oo

(Orchestral arrangement with violins, harp, and flutes)

At the end of the ballet, the audience stood and applauded. Ruby could feel tears at the back of her eyes. Lola and Zack could feel the same. Aileen and Maurice couldn't feel anything. They couldn't see what all the fuss was about, but they applauded just the same. They didn't want to appear the odd ones out, hypocritical as always.

After the show, they all went into the Theatre's bar for a drink. A while later, some of the ballet dancers wandered into the bar. Ruby looked out for Veronica and waved when she saw her.

Veronica kissed them all and thanked them for coming.

LOLA: 'You were wonderful, darling.'

VERONICA: 'Thanks, Mum.'

AILEEN: 'You've certainly come on leaps and bounds since we last saw you.'

MAURICE: 'Can I get you a drink, Veronica?'

VERONICA: 'No thanks. We are going to have to go I'm afraid. Ruby and I have a party to go to.'

LOLA: 'Off you go then, and enjoy yourselves. You deserve it.'

They watched them go.

AILEEN: 'You must be very proud of her, Lola.'

LOLA: 'I am. From what I hear, Ruby's doing pretty well too.'

Aileen didn't understand what she meant. She didn't see much of Ruby these days. The two girls had kept in touch. Ruby had told Veronica about Paolo and Veronica had told Ruby about Vladimir. She was dying to meet him.

The party was in the Green Room. Vladimir took hold of Ruby's hand and kissed it, a very theatrical gesture.

VLADIMIR: 'I hear much about you, Miss Ruby. It is an honour to meet you.'

Ruby giggled.

VERONICA: 'He's always like this. It's the way they teach them English in Russia – about a hundred years out of date!'

They both laughed at that.

VLADIMIR: 'My English is not good?'

RUBY: 'You do very well, Vladimir. Your English is a damn sight better than my Russian!'

VLADIMIR: 'You speak Russian?'

RUBY: 'No.'

VLADIMIR: 'I have much to learn about the English. They say one thing and mean another.'

Ruby and Veronica laughed again.

Gander, the new manager of the Duchess night club in York, had been kidding up Nathan for weeks, trying to get him to persuade Helen Row to bring her jazz band to his club. Gander knew Helen's band from when he was assistant manager at Ray Score's club in London. He had been there 20 years and would have remained there if he and his wife had not had a holiday in York and fell in love with the place.

Gander and his wife Edie were packing their bags at the end of their week's holiday in York when Edie said what was on both their minds.

EDIE: 'I know it's a pipe dream, love, but wouldn't it be marvellous if we could actually live here.'

Gander was at the hotel reception, settling their bill. A pretty receptionist was making it up for him.

GANDER: 'You look like a girl about town. Can you name all the nightclubs in York?

RECEPTIONIST: 'I can, yes. There's Fibbers, The Duchess, Kuda, Popworld, Flares. The Duchess is closed at the moment. They are doing it up. Someone new has bought it, I think.'

GANDER: 'Would you mind jotting those names down on a piece of paper for me.'

RECEPTIONIST: 'Of course, sir. There's your bill.'

When he got home, Gander looked up the night clubs on the internet. He composed an email with a brief CV and a few examples of his extensive client list and sent it to each of the night clubs. Two days later, he was checking his emails when he noticed one from BMG. BMG were the new owners of The Duke night club in York. They explained that they were in the process of refurbishing the club and were looking for a manager. They asked him to ring the phone number given and arrange an interview.

They offered Gander the job. They would have been fools not to; with Gander's experience and contacts, he was a big fish in a small pond. Managers from London didn't often relocate to York.

Nathan and Helen Row walked into Gander's office one Saturday lunchtime.

HELEN: 'Now then, Gander, you old rogue. What are you up to now?'

GANDER: 'Helen! What a pleasant surprise.'

HELEN: 'Not so much of the surprise. Nathan tells me you've been pestering the life out of him for weeks.'

GANDER: 'Well I may have made a few comments.'

HELEN: 'Are you serious about booking us here?'

GANDER: 'Of course I am.'

HELEN: 'OK. We are going to need at least two gigs, preferably three to make it worthwhile bringing the band from London. Can you arrange that?'

GANDER: 'Let's see, shall we?'

Gander picked up the phone and dialled Fibber's number. He laid it on with a trowel. Helen and Nathan winced at his glowing recommendation. They were going to have a lot to live up to. He put the phone down.

GANDER: 'That's one. Shall we try another?'

HELEN: 'Cool it a bit, Gander. We haven't played together for a while.'

Gander laughed.

GANDER: 'In for a penny, in for a pound.'

He secured three bookings.

HELEN: 'You had better come and stay with me in London, Nathan. We need to put some practice in.'

Ruby and her band, Ruby Kind, Margaret Eye and Dr Richard were all in the Duke night club eagerly awaiting Helen Row and her band. They were all in their sixties and seventies. Nathan was 72 but you wouldn't think so the way they played. They put some of the younger bands to shame with their energy. Ruby particularly liked *'Just One More'* that Helen sang as a duet with her trumpet player, Billy Eid.

JUST ONE MORE

I said hey it may be late but I'm still here with you
You said hey it may be late, but I'm still here with you
Well it's four o'clock in the morning
and I don't know what to do
You said hey you'll wait for me if only I'll wait for you

I said hey it may be late, it's time that I was gone
You said hey it may be late, it's time that I was gone
Well it's four o'clock in the morning,
and I should be moving on
You said hey you'll wait for me if only I won't be long

I said hey it may be late but there's time for just one more
You said hey it may be late but there's time for just one more
Well it's four o'clock in the morning
and I'm crawling on the floor
You said hey you'll drink with me but only just one more

Just one more, just one more
Just one more, just one more

Twenty-three

Yvonne had fallen off the wagon. She was back taking drugs. It started when she and her friend, Julie, from the squat, gate-crashed a party. They were in the Roman Bath pub in Parliament Street when they heard two boys talking about a party. They were on their third cider; their inhibitions were down. Julie came right out and asked the boys where the party was. The boys looked at them; their clothes looked shabby and their hair looked greasy but they were reasonable looking. The boys assumed they were students. Students were always hard up, they often looked like that.

BOY: 'What do you think, Zorba?'

JULIE: 'Zorba! What kind of name is that?'

They all laughed.

ZORBA: 'My dad was keen on Zorba the Greek.'

JULIE: 'Poor you!'

ZORBA: 'I quite like it, actually. It gets me noticed.'

JULIE: 'I guess it does. Come on then, Zorba, show us the way to this party. You can do your dance if you like.'

Julie linked arms with Zorba and they walked out of the pub and down the street. Yvonne and the other boy followed behind.

At the party, the boy soon got bored with Yvonne and wandered off to see his mates. There was no sign of Julie and Zorba.

Yvonne found herself in the kitchen, talking to a middle aged man. He was wearing an immaculate navy blue suit, crisp white shirt, and red and white tie. His dark hair was neatly cut with a touch of grey over the ears. His name was Geoff. Yvonne had had quite a bit to drink by this time and she was telling Geoff about her new York Tour. She was talking too much, but Geoff didn't seem to mind. In fact, he seemed interested in Yvonne's tour. He said he would like to go on it.

Yvonne left with Geoff. He took her home. They ended up in bed together, but Yvonne fell asleep. In the morning, Yvonne apologized. Geoff laughed.

GEOFF: 'It's usually the other way around and it's me who falls asleep.'

YVONNE: 'I'll make it up to you. I won't have so much to drink next time.'

GEOFF: 'OK I'm afraid I'm working for the next couple of nights but how do you fancy the Duke on Thursday?'

YVONNE: 'Great.'

GEOFF: 'I'll see you in there about 9 o'clock if that's alright.'

YVONNE: 'I'll be there. Looking forward to it, in fact.'

Yvonne thought she had better spruce herself up a bit if she was going to the Duke. She walked down Goodramgate and into the Oxfam shop. She bought the best clothes that she could afford for the princely sum of £15.

Geoff was already there, waiting for her when Yvonne walked into the Duke at 5 past 9. She liked that. She had heard that older men treated you better. They stayed until eleven then Geoff took Yvonne home. This time they did have sex. Afterwards, Geoff got up, walked out of the bedroom and came back with a square of silver paper. It was heroin.

GEOFF: 'Do you use this stuff?'

YVONNE: 'I used to.'

GEOFF: 'Don't let me get you into bad habits.'

Ruby Kind

YVONNE: 'I'll just try a bit.'

But as every addict will tell you, that's all it takes. Once you have tasted the forbidden fruit, you want more. Yvonne became a regular caller to Geoff's house. At first she thought there was more to it, but she soon realised there was no love there. Geoff was simply giving her drugs in return for sex.

One evening, Yvonne knocked on Geoff's door but there was no reply. She hung about a bit and tried again. Still no reply. She went back to the squat. She tried again the following day with the same result. She was getting a bit worried now and she needed a fix.

The next morning, she was up early and decided to go for a walk to take her mind off things. She came out of the squat, crossed Piccadilly and was about to set off into town when she noticed the newspaper seller's sign on the corner, in front of Lloyd's Bank. It said:

'Drug dealer arrested in dawn raid.'

Yvonne's first thought was Bobby. She bought a Press, turned round, and headed back inside the squat to read it. The article read:

'A man has been arrested in a dawn raid on a city taxi firm. Heroin with a street value in excess of £20,000 was found on the premises of Express Taxis in Haxby. Mr Geoffrey Blenkinhorn, owner of the taxi firm, was arrested and is helping police with their enquiries at Fulford Police headquarters. A spokesman for the police said they had had Mr Blenkinhorn under surveillance for several weeks, acting on a tip off that Express Taxis was a cover for a drug dealing operation.

Mr Blenkinhorn is described as 42, six foot tall and living in a large 4 bedroomed detached house in Greenshaw Drive, Haxby. Two other men were arrested with Mr Blenkinhorn but have since been released without charge.'

Yvonne didn't know much about Geoff. She didn't know his surname and she didn't know the name of his taxi firm. She didn't know how old he was either. She had been so blinkered by her own needs that she hadn't bothered to ask. But he did live in a large, detached house in Greenshaw Drive, Haxby. She didn't know how many bedrooms it had but it could be four. It was big enough. When she thought about it, he could very easily be a drug dealer. He always had plenty of the stuff, he drove a flash car and never bothered about money. And he had gone missing.

Ruby Kind

Yvonne's stomach turned over and she felt a bit sick. Was Geoffrey Blenkinhorn her Geoff? There was only one way to find out. She would have to get inside his house.

Yvonne went in search of Benny. She found him tucked away in a small room on the top floor. He was laid on the floor in his sleeping bag, fast asleep. Benny slept late on account of his nocturnal activities; he was a burglar. Yvonne had helped him out a few times when he needed someone small. Benny was over six foot and big with it, whereas Yvonne was only five foot two and thin as a rail. She could squeeze through small upstairs windows where Benny wouldn't stand a chance.

Yvonne shook Benny's shoulder.

YVONNE: 'Benny. Benny.'

BENNY: 'Wha ... Oh, it's you, Yvonne. Is everything alright?'

YVONNE: 'I need to borrow your cutter, Benny.'

Benny lifted himself up on his elbow.

BENNY: 'Branching out on your own, are you?'

YVONNE: 'Not exactly.'

BENNY: 'Do you want a hand?'

YVONNE: 'No, it's alright. I can manage.'

BENNY: 'Suit yourself. It's in my jacket pocket, on the right.'

Yvonne reached into the jacket pocket and pulled out a little glass cutter.

BENNY: 'I want it back mind.'

YVONNE: 'Don't worry. I'll have it back to you well before nightfall.'

Yvonne caught a bus to Haxby and began the long walk up Greenshaw Drive. It was a long street. When she reached Geoff's house, she walked up to the front door and rang the bell, just in case. There was no reply. She went round to the back of the house. The garden was surrounded by a tall leylandii hedge. It was very private. The garden was a great expanse of grass.

Yvonne cut a four inch circle of glass out of the kitchen window, using the glass cutter as Benny had shown her. She opened the window and climbed inside. First of all, she decided to check out the bedrooms. There were indeed four, but there was nothing to indicate who Geoff was. Downstairs in the lounge, against one wall was a large old sideboard. She opened the top left hand drawer. It looked to be full of bills. She flicked through the bills. They were all addressed to Mr G Blenkinhorn. She opened more of the drawers and found a stack of business cards with 'Express Taxis, Haxby' printed on them, and a phone number.

Yvonne sat down on the settee to think. So her Geoff was the Geoffrey Blenkinhorn that they had arrested. He was a drug dealer. What should she do now? Her next thought was inevitable. Where did he keep his stash? She resumed her search, trying to keep the panic down that was threatening to rise up and engulf her. In one of the kitchen drawers, she found Geoff's car keys. She slipped them into her pocket. She couldn't exactly say why; she couldn't drive. It was just an impulse thing.

After about a half hour of fruitless searching, her nerves could stand it no longer and she climbed out of the kitchen window and forced herself to walk slowly away from the house, when all her instincts were telling her to run as fast as she could.

Back at the squat, Yvonne bumped into Bobby.

BOBBY: 'Hi, Yvonne. How are you doing?'

YVONNE: 'OK. How's the DJing business?'

BOBBY: 'Great. Would you believe I've got a party at the Merchant Adventurers Hall for a load of solicitors no less.'

YVONNE: 'Blimey. Mind how you go. I would leave your Es at home.'

BOBBY: 'Too right.'

Yvonne looked down at the ground and shuffled her feet.

BOBBY: 'Are you sure you're alright, Yvonne? You look kind of strung up.'

YVONNE: 'I need a fix, Bobby. My source has dried up.'

BOBBY: 'I thought you were in rehab.'

YVONNE: 'I was, but it's really hard, you know. You've no idea what it's like till you've been through it. I just couldn't do it Bobby.'

BOBBY: 'OK. I can get you some stuff but it will take a couple of days. Would you like some pot to put you on?'

YVONNE: 'Wouldn't mind.'

Bobby took a small bag out of his pocket and handed it to Yvonne.

BOBBY: 'I'm sorry I have to say this Yvonne, with you being a mate, but business is business. This is going to cost. Can you afford it?'

Yvonne remembered Geoff's car keys. She took them out of her pocket and put them in Bobby's hand.

YVONNE: 'Did you see the drug dealer in the paper that's been arrested?'

BOBBY: 'Yeah, gave me a bit of a turn.'

YVONNE: 'Me too. That's the keys to his car. It's a BMW seven something or other.'

BOBBY: 'Great! I've always wanted a beamer.'

YVONNE: 'Sell it on Bobby. As far away from York as you can manage. The police know whose car it is. They'll stop you and want to know how you got it.'

BOBBY: 'Right. Pity. Where is it?'

Yvonne gave him the address.

Ruby and Yvonne had a regular date every Wednesday lunchtime. Yvonne sold the Big Issue outside W H Smiths in Coney Street on

Wednesdays. It was where they had first met. They usually went for a coffee in Starbucks. They went for nights out together too, but that was just one-offs, whereas Wednesdays were regular.

Ruby walked down Coney Street Wednesday lunchtime. Yvonne wasn't there. She hung around for a bit then carried on to the Library. When she come back, Yvonne still wasn't there. There was no time to go to the squat, she had an appointment with Mr Crabtree at 2 o'clock. She would go after school. Something must have prevented Yvonne from being at her usual pitch. Maybe she was ill or something.

Ruby let herself into the squat at 4.30. There was no one about. She walked from room to room. There wasn't a soul. She climbed the stairs to the next floor. She could hear a humming noise coming from the ballroom. She opened one of the double doors. In the middle of the White Swan Hotel's old ballroom, all 16 members of the squat were sat down, cross-legged, in a circle. In the middle of the circle, joss sticks burned. Ruby could smell the sweet scent. Ruby looked closer at the people in the circle. Their arms were stretched out and rested on their knees. Their thumbs and forefingers were pressed together and they all made the yogic chant: 'Ohmmm.'

Ruby had been a regular visitor to the squat for about 6 months. Nothing like this had ever happened before. Everyone seemed to have their eyes closed. Then she noticed Julie looking at her and their eyes met. Julie nodded her head, got up, and left the circle. She took hold of Ruby's arm and led her into the corridor.

JULIE: 'I'm afraid I've got some bad news, Ruby. Yvonne is dead.'

RUBY: 'Dead? I don't understand. What happened?'

JULIE: 'Overdose.'

RUBY: 'But I thought she was off drugs. She was off drugs. She told me!'

JULIE: 'That's what we thought too. But apparently not. There's no doubt. It's definitely an overdose.'

RUBY: 'I can't believe it. She had everything to live for. She had written her new tour. She took me on it. It's great. She was talking about going back to university.'

Silence.

JULIE: 'We're having a wake; would you like to join us?

Julie and Ruby joined the others in the circle. Ruby's mind was in turmoil. She listened to the chant: 'Ohmmm'. After a while, she joined in. It was strangely comforting.

Jack and Ruby were stood in the garden outside the Crematorium after Yvonne's funeral. Neither of them were in any hurry to leave.

JACK: 'It's such a waste, Ruby. Everything was just coming right. She had had such a struggle but she finally seemed to have turned a corner. She's written a completely new historical tour of York. It's great. Much better than mine. I honestly believe that she was some kind of genius when it came to history.'

RUBY: 'I know. She took me on the tour. She fired my interest in history. I can't get enough of it now. Are you going to run Yvonne's tour?

JACK: 'I'd like to. But now Yvonne's gone, I've no one to take it.'

RUBY: 'I'll take it. I'll take it and I don't want paying. Give the money to the rehab project.'

JACK: 'That's good of you, Ruby. I was thinking of donating so much to the rehab project. It's the least I can do in Yvonne's memory. Don't ever get involved in drugs, Ruby. I couldn't stand another one of these things.'

RUBY: 'Yvonne told me all about drugs. I don't need to experiment with them. I know what they are like. There are no good points to taking drugs, only bad. If people knew what drugs did to them, no one would take them. Like smoking, they would just die a death.'

Twenty-four

Ruby Kind were the support act to The Drumbeats at the Duchess night club in York. It was their first proper weekend gig at the Duchess: Friday and Saturday night, a step up for them. Ruby Kind had finished their set. The Drumbeats were on stage now. Ruby was sat in the audience with Lenny Ravowich, The Drumbeats manager.

LENNY: 'Have you given any more thought to turning professional, Ruby?'

RUBY: 'It's kind of you to ask, Lenny, but we have a way to go yet. We've only been together for just under a year. We need to expand our repertoire and I maybe ought to try my hand at writing something.'

LENNY: 'I'm not being kind, Ruby. I'm a businessman. I tell you, you could turn professional any time you wanted. As for your band, yes there is room for improvement there, but it will come. You just need to play more.'

Lenny took a card out of his pocket and gave it to Ruby.

LENNY: 'If you change your mind, give me a ring. Can I have your phone number?'

Ruby Kind

Ruby gave him her phone number at the farm. When Ruby put her make-up on and got dressed up, you could take her to be anything from 20 to 30 years old. Lenny didn't know she was still a school girl. He thought she worked on a farm, as that was what Ruby had told him. He thought her name was Ruby Kind, the same as her band. Again, Ruby didn't correct him.

Tony Endling was on holiday, skiing with his family in Switzerland. Tony was the keyboard player in The Drumbeats. They had snatched a quick break during a lull in the band's gigs. They didn't like taking the children out of school, but they were only young: six and nine, it wouldn't do them any harm. It wasn't as if they were studying for exams. Tony and his family liked to ski, even six year old Robin could whiz down the slopes. It was the beginning of December. The Drumbeats would be working all over Christmas. It was their busiest time of the year. For Tony and his family, this was their Christmas.

Tony was a very good skier. He liked to ski off piste, in fresh, white, virgin snow. Only the most experienced could do that. It was considered a bit dangerous. The mountains were unpredictable. There was always a risk of avalanche, but it was like a drug to Tony. He couldn't resist it. In fact, he loved it. Tony was up early: 6 o'clock. He was going up Klosters Weissflohgifel with four other men, one of whom was an instructor. He was excited. He left his family asleep in their log cabin and stepped out into the cold, crisp, morning air. He felt good to be alive.

They caught the ski lift up Weissflohgifel and walked the rest of the way to the top. Tony set off first downhill. On these slopes, you could easily get up to 60 miles an hour. He swooped round an outcrop of rock, turned left, and leapt into the air over a sudden drop. His ski hit something, probably a rock hidden by the deep snow, and he went down heavily, landing on his right side. He heard the 'crack' and felt a sharp pain shoot through his right arm. The others shot down and stopped beside him. The instructor carried a first aid kit, but you didn't need to be a trained first aider to see that Tony's arm was broken. The Instructor formed a sling and gently eased Tony's arm into it. Two of them helped him to his feet and guided him down the mountain, one on each side. They took him back to

Ruby Kind

his log cabin and the Instructor called an ambulance.

Tony was in Davos Hospital. They had put a pot on his arm; obviously, he wasn't going to be able to play keyboards. He made the dreaded call to Lenny, who took it very well, considering they were coming up to their busiest time at Christmas. Lenny told him to look after himself and not to worry about the band. He would sort that. He rang off saying: 'Love to Rachel and the kids.'

Lenny was famous for being able to think fast in a tight corner. He just went into overdrive. Several possibilities flashed through his mind. They could not afford to cancel the Christmas gigs. He needed a replacement for Tony, fast. Lenny rang a couple of session musicians that he knew. They were booked solid for Christmas, as he had expected. He sat back in his chair, closed his eyes, and let his mind wander. A little voice at the back of his head said: 'What about Ruby? What about Ruby?' He was sure she could do it, but she would be playing with her band over Christmas, the same as everyone else. But would she prefer to play with The Drumbeats? There was only one way to find out.

Lenny rang Ruby's number. He got Jonah's answer machine. He decided not to leave a message, he would try again later. He rang again at ten past six. This time, Ruby answered.

RUBY: 'Hello Lenny. Happy Christmas.'

LENNY: 'Happy Christmas, Ruby. How are things with you?'

RUBY: 'I'm fine, Lenny but I'm wondering why you have called. You have never called me before. You must have something on your mind.'

LENNY: 'You see right through me, Ruby, as usual. Yes, I do have a reason for ringing you.'

RUBY: 'Come on, Lenny. Spit it out.'

Lenny liked Ruby's blunt talking. She was down to earth, something you didn't get very often in the music business. Most people had an ego.

LENNY: 'Tony Endling has broken his arm skiing. Do you know Tony? He plays the keyboards.'

RUBY: 'In The Drumbeats?'

LENNY: 'Yes. I need someone to stand in for him over the Christmas period. I could probably find someone else once Christmas is over. Christmas is one of our busiest times. The trouble is it's everybody else's busiest time as well. I'm having great difficulty filling the vacancy.'

RUBY: 'You want me to play the keyboards in The Drumbeats?'

LENNY: 'Yes.'

RUBY: 'Have you lost your mind, Lenny? This is a professional band you're talking about. How would I keep up with them?'

LENNY: 'Don't put yourself down, Ruby. As I've said to you before, you could turn professional any time you wanted. You can do this. I've seen you play. I wouldn't have rung you if I didn't think you could do it.'

RUBY: 'But we've got gigs booked over Christmas: four confirmed and two definite 'maybes'. There may be a few more before the holiday is over. I can't just say to Ruby Kind: 'Sorry guys, I've had a better offer. I'm dumping you.' I am their leader. They would be devastated if I did that and what about all those people at the Christmas parties. What are they going to say if the band doesn't turn up? We have spent a long time building our reputation. If we cancel the parties, it will be shattered.'

LENNY: 'Sorry, Ruby, I shouldn't have asked. It was unfair of me. Of course you have your own commitments. I should have known you wouldn't want to do it.'

RUBY: 'No, no, no. You don't understand. I want to do it, but I just don't see how I can. How long have I got?'

LENNY: 'I'd really like you for the Westminster Hall gig on the 23rd. I know it's short notice. I can send the music to you by courier. You'll have it by first thing tomorrow morning. Does that give you enough time to learn it?'

RUBY: 'I don't have to learn it; I'll just play from the music.'

LENNY: 'That's what I was hoping you'd say.'

RUBY: 'I'll have to think about this, Lenny. See if I can work something out. I appreciate you ringing me. It's a golden opportunity to work with a professional outfit. I just wish you had given me a bit more notice.'

LENNY: 'Sorry, Ruby. I don't suppose Tony's too pleased with his arm in plaster.'

RUBY: 'Give me your phone number again, Lenny. I don't know what I've done with your card.'

Lenny gave her his phone number and she promised to ring him back.

Ruby Kind

Ruby was still pondering her problem the next morning at breakfast. Jonah was up before her, cooking bacon and eggs. That usually meant he was after something; Ruby usually cooked the breakfast.

JONAH: 'I'm going to see Marie for Christmas, Ruby, in Venice. I'll probably stay the full fortnight. Will you be alright here on your own?'

The cogs in Ruby's brain whirred round: The Drumbeats, Ruby Kind, Miss Eyeball, Paolo.

RUBY: 'Possibly.'

JONAH: 'Is everything alright, Ruby? You look far away.'

RUBY: 'It might be, Uncle Jonah. You've given me an idea. It's out of this world, but it might just work.'

Ruby rang Lenny. It was a quarter to seven.

LENNY: 'Jeez, Ruby. What time do you call this?'

RUBY: 'Sorry. We rise early on the farm. Can you tell me the dates of the gigs you want me to play?'

LENNY: 'Err, yes. I'll get the diary.'

Lenny read out the dates.

RUBY: 'I can't make the two mid-week dates, but I may be able to do the others. I've got to see someone about covering for me.'

LENNY: 'Are you thinking about commuting?'

RUBY: 'Sort of, I'm going to Italy.'

LENNY: 'Italy?!'

RUBY: 'Yeah, my boyfriend lives there. I'll fly out and see him during the week and fly back at weekends to play with The Drumbeats. Only I'm going to need some money, Lenny, for the plane fares. How much are you paying me?'

LENNY: 'I don't know. I haven't worked it out.'

RUBY: 'I know it's early morning, Lenny, but you should be more on the ball than that.'

LENNY: 'Sorry. You're right, of course. I'll just get my calculator.'

There was silence for a while.

LENNY: 'How does five thousand pounds sound?'

RUBY: 'Fine, but I'll need half of it in advance.'

LENNY: 'No problem, would you like it in cash?'

RUBY: 'That's a good idea. It will save messing around with the bank.'

LENNY: 'I was being sarcastic.'

RUBY: 'Sorry. Never was good with sarcasm. I can't see it. The cash is a good idea though.'

LENNY: 'You'll do it then, Ruby?'

RUBY: 'I don't know yet. I've got a few more things to sort out, but it's not looking as impossible as it was.'

Ruby knocked on the Staff Common Room door. It was 8.30. Assembly didn't start until nine. Mr Crabtree opened the door.

MR CRABTREE: 'Come in, Ruby. You're early. Actually it's very fortuitous. I have acquired a very good book about the Romans. I was going to show it to you. You can borrow it if you like, after I'm finished with it.'

RUBY: 'Thanks, Mr Crabtree. I'd like that. Actually, it's Miss Eye I'm after.'

MR CRABTREE: 'Miss Eye? What's the time. 8.30. She should be here any time now. Come in. We'll look at the book while you're waiting.'

Margaret Eye walked into the Common Room.

MARGARET: 'Morning, Ted. Morning Ruby. What's this, another project?'

RUBY: 'I wanted to ask you a favour, Miss. Quite a big favour, actually.'

MARGARET: 'Go on then, Ruby. You've got my attention.'

RUBY: 'I've been invited to play the keyboards for The Drumbeats over Christmas. Their keyboard player has broken his arm. But I can't do it because Ruby Kind are booked to play over Christmas. I can't just up sticks and leave them without a keyboard player. Besides, I'm their leader. I want to play with them.'

MARGARET: 'Unless you can find someone to stand in for you.'

RUBY: 'That's right.'

Ruby never ceased to be amazed how quickly Miss Eyeball worked things out. She was very bright.

MARGARET: 'I'd be delighted to cover for you, Ruby. Dr Richard is writing a book. He has a deadline to meet. It looks as though he'll be hard at it all Christmas. I'll be left to my own devices. I was thinking about doing some decorating, but I would much rather play in your band. If there's one thing

I've missed since I left the orchestra, it is the buzz of a live performance. There is nothing like it.'

MR CRABTREE: 'Fortuitous again, Ruby. Maybe we should make that your middle name.'

RUBY: 'Ruby Fortuitous Fish – has a sort of intellectual quality about it, don't you think?'

They all laughed at that.

MARGARET: 'You are a lucky girl having the opportunity to play with a professional band like The Drumbeats, Ruby. It will be good experience. You should learn a lot.'

RUBY: 'That's what I thought, but I must handle Ruby Kind carefully. Can you come to our rehearsals on Saturday morning at the barn, Miss?'

MARGARET: 'Yes, of course.'

Ruby left her band in the barn and went into the farmhouse to fetch something. She came back carrying a brief case, accompanied by Miss Eyeball.

RUBY: 'I've got a favour to ask you guys. I've been invited to play the keyboards for The Drumbeats over Christmas. Their keyboard player has broken his arm. I was going to turn them down when Miss

Eye offered to cover for me. I know we've all put a lot of work into this Christmas's preparations but this is a big opportunity for me to play in a professional band. It's not something I expected to come along so soon. I will only do it if we all agree that I should do it. It's up to you guys.'

SILENCE.

EVAN: 'How come they picked on you?'

RUBY: 'I'd like to think it was my brilliant talent, but it was probably Hobson's choice. Lenny Ravowich, The Drumbeats manager rang me up and asked me to do it. He did admit that he was having trouble finding anyone else.'

MARGARET: 'Don't put yourself down, Ruby. Lenny wouldn't have asked you if he didn't think you could do it. You are a very talented musician and every person in this group knows that.'

EVAN: 'Is Lenny what's-his-name that big foreign looking guy with the goatee beard?'

RUBY: 'Yeah, that's him.'

EVAN: 'He spoke to me once. He said if I worked hard, I had the makings of a good guitarist. Cheeky sod. I already am a good guitarist.'

Ruby laughed.

RUBY: 'He has said the same sort of thing to me. It makes you angry. It makes you work hard, just to show him. That's what he wants, of course.'

EVAN: 'I guess you're right. I'm sorry, Miss Eye. We all know what a great musician you are. You've taught us all. Of course you can stand in for Ruby. It's just a bit disappointing – we are Ruby's band. If it wasn't for her, we wouldn't be here.'

MARGARET: 'I know, Evan, but you've got to look at the bigger picture. Ruby is going to gain valuable experience and she'll come back with a whole new repertoire. Show them the music, Ruby.'

Ruby opened her briefcase and took out a stack of sheet music.

RUBY: 'It's all there, complete arrangements. It would take me hours and hours of work, listening to records, writing the music and it's much better than I could do.'

MARGARET: 'Evan has done all the talking so far. What do the rest of you think?'

KIRSTY: 'I think it's very exciting. I wish I was going with you, Ruby.'

JASON: 'I can see both sides. I don't have strong feelings either way. If you want to do it, Ruby, go for it.'

EVAN: 'This music is amazing. I may have to change my opinion.'

MARGARET: 'Ade, you're very quiet. What do you think?'

ADE: 'I just think that once Ruby has seen the bright lights, she'll forget all about us.'

MARGARET: 'What are you afraid of, Ade? Ruby's ambition? It's Ruby's ambition that has got the band this far. When she comes back from London, and she will come back, Ade, she will know exactly where she wants this band to go, because she will have seen what can be done. If you want to be part of that future, you had better shape up.'

SILENCE

RUBY: 'Well, that's cleared the air nicely. You are a star, Miss. I've wanted to give them a good bollocking a few times. They just leave everything to me.'

She was laughing. Pretty soon, they were all laughing.

RUBY: 'Can we have a show of hands. All those in favour of me playing with The Drumbeats over Christmas, raise your right hand.'

They all raised their right arm, except Evan, who raised his left.

RUBY: 'I think you frightened them all to death, Miss.'

Twenty-five

Ruby had one more phone call to make, one last piece of the jigsaw to put into place, but it was the most important piece. If this didn't work out, there would be no point in anything else. She rang Paolo.

RUBY: 'Hallo, Paolo. It's me. How are you doing?'

PAOLO: 'Aah Ruby. You ring me. This is good, very good.'

RUBY: 'Paolo, I've got to play with the band over the two Christmas weekends, but I can come and see you during the week if that's alright.'

Paolo said something in excited, rapid Italian that Ruby couldn't catch. Sophia came on the line.

SOPHIA: 'What have you said to Paolo, Ruby? He is running round the room with his arms outstretched imitating an aeroplane!'

Ruby laughed.

RUBY: 'I've just asked him if I can come and see him over Christmas.'

SOPHIA: 'I think it's safe to say that he is looking forward to it. Is Jonah coming too?'

RUBY: 'No, he's going to see Marie in Venice.'

SOPHIA: 'It seems that everyone is holding hands except me.'

RUBY: 'Is there no one special in your life right now, Sophia?'

SOPHIA: 'Well, there is this doctor that I am quite keen on. He's ten years older than me, but he has beautiful, gentle hands.'

RUBY: 'Oh yeah, and where have those beautiful, gentle hands been, Sophia?'

They both laughed.

SOPHIA: 'That would be telling. See you Christmas, Ruby.'

RUBY: 'See you Christmas, Sophia. Bye, love to Paolo.'

Ruby told Jonah exactly what she was doing for Christmas but she just told her parents that she was going to Italy. They weren't interested anyway; they were too busy with their own lives.

Ruby enjoyed all of the gigs she played with the Drumbeats, but the one that stood out was Ray

Score's Club. They were the support act to Jim Sage, the legendary Lee Zopper guitarist. Ray Score was a jazz trumpeter. His band were nothing special but Ray was also a good businessman. He started his club in 1959.

Now it was an important part of the London night life. They still played jazz, but nowadays they featured other types of music too: the blues, rock guitar, classical guitar, flamenco guitar, but their hallmark was quality. If you wanted good music, Ray Score's was the place to be.

Whilst they were all in Italy, Sophia had asked Mr Bellini to try again with the Vatican Bank and see if they would allow them to open Bruno's safety deposit box. Mr Bellini had tried a couple of times. He had written to the Bank. He had attended a meeting with a Bank Official and been forced to hand over all his documents, including Bruno's will and the Magrioni family tree. Like a fool, he hadn't made a copy. He tried to persuade the Official to let him make a copy but the Official had the documents in his hand and wasn't about to give them back. He said if Mr Bellini really wanted to open Mr Magrioni's safety deposit box, he had no choice but to leave him the original documents. He expected The Pope would want to see them.

Mr Bellini agreed and crossed his fingers that he would get the documents back. He still had his copy of Bruno's will but if they lost the family tree, Sophia and Ruby would have to start all over again. It didn't bear thinking about.

Mr Bellini rang the Vatican Bank Official that he had been dealing with. He was positively effusive, congratulating him and his clients in tracing the Magrioni family tree and discovering the safety deposit box here in the Vatican Bank. The Pope was very pleased that one of the old deposit boxes was going to be opened. It happened so rarely. Mr Bellini could hardly believe his ears. This was the man who was suspicious, cold, unfriendly, who looked at him as if he was trying to rob the bank. He had had a personality transplant. The official was saying that he would send him a letter of authority which he should present when he and his clients entered the bank and he, the official, would take them to Bruno Magrioni's safety deposit box personally.

Mr Bellini picked up the phone to ring Sophia. Then put it down again. He didn't entirely trust the official. He would wait until he received the letter.

Who knows, the man might change again and have another incarnation. Anything was possible.

But the letter did arrive, 3 days later and it was signed by The Pope.

Mr Bellini gave Jonah the key. He inserted it into the lock in the deposit box door. The official inserted another key into the second lock on the door. They turned their keys: 'Click, click'. Jonah took hold of the handle and pulled the door open.

Inside was another box which was so heavy that it took four of them to lift down. They placed it on the floor and stared at it in disbelief. There were gold cups, gold plates with big, fat, rubies. There was gold and diamond necklaces, a 3 inch gold orb with a central band studded with diamonds, emeralds, rubies, sapphires. Then there was the silver.

Jonah broke the spell.

JONAH: 'It looks like Blackbeard's treasure!'

They all laughed at that.

RUBY: 'I don't think even Blackbeard could have amassed all that lot!'

Ruby Kind

Julian and Rosalind, two antique experts were cataloguing the contents of Bruno's house for Misties, the London Antique Auctioneers. Mr Bellini had suggested to Sophia and the others that whatever they decided to do with the house, either sell it or rent it out to holidaymakers, the contents would have to be sold. They were too valuable to be left where they were. The four friends agreed. Julian and Rosalind had been there several weeks. It was a big job. They had discussed it with their boss and suggested to Mr Bellini that they split the contents into four separate auctions, to be spread over the course of a year. This way, they could build up interest from one auction to the other, saving the best stuff until last. Mr Bellini agreed; so did Sophia, Paolo, Jonah and Ruby.

Mr Bellini asked Julian and Rosalind to come with them when they opened Bruno's safety deposit box at the Vatican Bank. Rosalind opened her briefcase and took out some electronic scales and a hand held computer notebook. She set about weighing the gold. Julian screwed in an eyepiece and examined the jewels. When they had finished with each piece, they handed them to the others. After an hour,

Julian took out his eyepiece and looked at Mr Bellini.

JULIAN: 'This is going to take quite some time.'

MR BELLINI: 'I know.'

He turned to the others.

MR BELLINI: 'What do you want us to do with this guys?'

JONAH: 'What do you think it will be worth, Julian?'

JULIAN: 'It's hard to say. Some of the items look like they are from Ancient Greece and Rome. If I'm right, they should be in a museum. I suppose one has to put a price on them but really they are priceless.'

RUBY: 'Come on, Julian. Take an educated guess. No one is going to hold you to it.'

Julian ran his hand through his thick, blond hair and blew out his cheeks.

JULIAN: 'Where are you up to on the gold, Rosalind?'

ROSALIND: '£237,429. But it would be sacrilege to melt down this stuff. It is worth far more in its original state.'

JULIAN: 'That's true, of course, but it gives us a base figure. All I can say is that you are looking at millions. We are only a quarter of the way down the box and there must be two or three millions worth there at least. If some of these pieces do have historical importance, as I think they do, there is no ceiling. They could just take off.'

RUBY: 'I think we should leave them where they are. They are safe here. They have appreciated over the years. They are better than money in the bank. I say we concentrate on getting the house contents ready for auction and put these things back until we have time to deal with them properly.'

SOPHIA: 'I think that's a good idea.'

JONAH: 'So do I.'

Sophia translated for Paolo who also agreed. So they put everything back into the Safety Deposit Box and locked it up.

By the end of the first auction, they had raised £12,748,286. Mr Bellini was ready to distribute the money to the claimants. He asked Ruby again if her mother had signed the claim form. He managed to keep the annoyance out of his voice, even though this was the third time he had asked.

RUBY: 'Sorry, Mr Bellini. I'll have a word with her as soon as I can.'

Ruby had to make an appointment to see her parents, such were their busy lives.

They were sat in the lounge. Aileen and Maurice on the sofa and Ruby in the armchair, facing them.

AILEEN: 'Come on, Ruby. What's all this about. I don't see why you have to be so secretive.'

RUBY: 'I've been researching the Magrioni family tree with Uncle Jonah. We have two cousins: Sophia and Paolo Magrioni who live in Pisa, Italy. They own a farm. The Magrionis have lived in Pisa for a very long time, but they didn't originate from there. They came from Venice …'

Aileen's eyes glazed over.

AILEEN: 'What's all this got to do with me, Ruby? I don't like you wallowing in the past. A young girl like you should be looking to the future, making plans: where are you going to university? What are you going to study? And so on.'

Ruby tried again.

RUBY: 'We've drawn up a family tree.'

She opened Sophia's briefcase and took out the roll of wallpaper and all the certificates and placed them down on the coffee table.

RUBY: 'As you can see, we have traced the family tree right back to Bruno Magrioni in 1576.'

Aileen's eyes stared wide at the coffee table.

AILEEN: 'How on earth have you found the time to do all this? You should be studying for your exams.'

RUBY: 'I didn't do it on my own. Sophia helped me.'

AILEEN: 'I blame Jonah for this. He must have encouraged you. Wait till I see him.'

RUBY: 'You don't understand, Mum. Bruno left a will. You need to sign this claim form.'

AILEEN: 'I'm not signing no form. You hear about people who sign forms that they don't understand. They get into all sorts of trouble. I hope you haven't signed any forms, Ruby.'

Ruby knew when she was beat. She packed everything away in the briefcase. Her Father said nothing throughout. She looked at him. He just shook his head.

Aileen burst into the farmhouse kitchen where Jonah and Ruby were having their breakfast the following morning. She flew at Jonah.

AILEEN: 'What the devil do you think you are playing at, Jonah, encouraging Ruby to trace your stupid family tree. Don't you know that this is the most important year of her life. Her A level results will determine what she does for her whole future career and you've got her neglecting her books, working on this wild goose chase.'

Jonah didn't say anything, he just waited until she ran out of steam.

JONAH: 'You're a stupid woman, Aileen. You always have been and you always will be. How you came to give birth to a brilliant child like Ruby is beyond me. But I thank God that you did. It is your only redeeming feature. Now, if you don't mind, I've got a field of wheat to cut.'

Jonah bundled Aileen out the door and stuffed her into her car. She sped off, spinning the wheels on the gravel. Jonah and Ruby watched her go.

RUBY: 'Funny, she didn't insist that I came home.'

JONAH: 'Yeah, I thought that. She seems to accept that you live here now.'

RUBY: 'What do we do now?'

JONAH: 'I don't know, I'll have a think while I'm driving the combine. It's very soothing driving the combine up and down. I often have my best thoughts then.'

It was late when Jonah rang Mr Bellini at home that evening. He didn't get in from the fields until after 8 o'clock.

JONAH: 'Sorry I'm ringing so late, Mr Bellini. I've been on the combine harvester getting the wheat in.'

MR BELLINI: 'Don't apologise, Jonah. I quite understand. A farmer's life is a busy one. Are you ringing me about your sister's claim form?'

JONAH: 'I am. I'm afraid she is not going to sign it, Mr Bellini. I know it's unbelievable but you have to know Aileen to understand. She is a one-off. Ruby has tried to explain it to her, but she mistrusts forms and refuses to sign.'

MR BELLINI: 'Very well. I have no choice but to proceed without her. I will issue the cheques tomorrow morning.'

JONAH: 'Don't worry about Aileen, Mr Bellini. I'll make sure she gets her share, even if I have to dump a suitcase full of twenty pound notes on her doorstep!'

They laughed at that.

Four days later, two letters arrived at the farm, one for Jonah and one for Ruby. They were both postmarked Venice. Jonah opened his first. Inside was a brief covering letter from Mr Bellini and a cheque for £3,187,072.

JONAH: 'I knew it was coming, but it's a shock when you see it in black and white.'

Ruby opened her envelope. She had the same.

RUBY: 'What are we going to do about Mum?'

JONAH: 'Oh yeah. I meant to tell you. I had an idea when I was driving the combine. It should be fun.'

Twenty-six

Saturday morning, Maurice was playing golf as usual and Aileen was having a rare day off. So she was in the house on her own. Jonah and Ruby parked the Land Rover round the corner from Aileen's house and got out. When they reached Aileen's gate, Jonah pulled on a Mickey Mouse mask and Ruby pulled on a Donald Duck mask. In his left hand, Jonah carried a duck egg blue, plastic, Samsonite suitcase. In his right hand he carried a gun that he had bought yesterday from Toys"R"Us.

Jonah rang Aileen's bell. She opened the door and stared at Mickey Mouse and Donald Duck. Then she noticed the gun.

JONAH: 'Top of the morning to ya, Missus. Would you be making a contribution to the wee orphans?'

Jonah had decided to be Irish.

Aileen made to close the door, but Jonah had his foot in and pushed through. Aileen retreated to the lounge, her face pale, and her eyes wide.

AILEEN: 'What do you want?'

JONAH: 'Oh, just the usual Missus. Money and jewellery.'

He placed the suitcase on the floor.

Aileen snatched up her handbag, took out her purse and handed Jonah £45.

AILEEN: 'I don't keep much money in the house. That's all I've got.'

JONAH: 'Where is your jewellery?'

AILEEN: 'Upstairs in my dressing table drawer, but there's not much.'

JONAH: 'Off you go, Sheila.'

RUBY: 'Will do, Blue.'

Jonah winced underneath his Mickey Mouse mask. Ruby couldn't do an Irish accent so she had decided to be Australian. She knew what they sounded like from watching Neighbours.

Two minutes later, Ruby came running downstairs and into the lounge.

RUBY: 'There's two rozzers coming down the street, mate!'

JONAH: 'Quick, leg it girl.'

RUBY: 'What about the suitcase, mate?'

JONAH: 'Leave it, it will only slow us down. We'll come back for it later.'

They ran out of the house slamming the front door. Halfway down the path they ripped off their masks, ran to the Land Rover, jumped in, and sped off, laughing.

JONAH: 'What do you think she will do?'

RUBY: 'Ring Dad. She won't touch the suitcase.'

JONAH: 'I'd love to be a fly on the wall.'

RUBY: 'Me too.'

Aileen did ring Maurice. She rang his mobile. He was on the third tee, lining up a difficult 15 yard put when his phone rang.

GOLFER: 'I thought we had agreed to turn off those things.'

MAURICE: 'Sorry. It's Aileen. I'll have to take it.'

MAURICE: 'Hello, Aileen. Is everything alright?'

AILEEN: 'No, Maurice. Everything is not alright. We have been robbed. I want you to come home.'

MAURICE: 'I'll be home as soon as I can Aileen, I'm on the third tee …'

Aileen shouted into the phone.

AILEEN: 'I DON'T CARE ABOUT YOUR BLOODY GOLF, MAURICE! GET YOURSELF HOME IF YOU KNOW WHAT'S GOOD FOR YOU.'

Aileen had shouted so loud that Maurice had to hold the phone away from his ear. His golfing partner heard what she said.

GOLFER: 'Trouble at mill, eh Maurice? There'll be no nookie for you tonight.'

They laughed, but Maurice wasn't laughing inside. He didn't like the sound of Aileen. He didn't like the sound of her at all.

When Maurice got home, Aileen was sat on the edge of the settee, staring at the suitcase.

MAURICE: 'Right, Aileen. Tell me exactly what happened.'

AILEEN: 'There were two of them. They had Disney masks on: Mickey Mouse and Donald Duck. The man sounded Irish and the woman sounded Australian. The woman noticed two policemen coming down the street and they ran off, leaving the suitcase behind. They said they would come back for it.'

MAURICE: 'Did they hurt you?'

AILEEN: 'No. They didn't lay a finger on me, but the man had a gun. He pointed it at me.'

MAURICE: 'What's in the suitcase?'

AILEEN: 'I don't know. I daren't touch it.'

Maurice walked over to the suitcase and picked it up. It wasn't heavy. He flicked the catches. To his surprise, it opened. It wasn't locked. He put it onto the table and lifted the lid. It looked to be full of twenty pound notes.

AILEEN: 'Oh my God! They'll kill us, Maurice. We must call the police.'

Maurice wasn't fazed by the sight of all that cash. As a Building Society Manager, he had handled cash all his working life. He knew how difficult it was to obtain that amount of cash.

MAURICE: 'Let's not be too hasty here, Aileen. We need to think this through. We need to know what we are dealing with. It could be counterfeit. We need to examine it, count it. I don't understand how a couple of burglars come to have such a large amount of cash. They can't have got it from a burglary; it's too neat. There would be notes of different denominations. This looks like it's all twenty pound notes.

Aileen was recovering from her panic and starting to think too.

AILEEN: 'Yes. I see what you mean. The man asked me for money and jewellery. He took £45 off me. Why would he do that if he had all that cash?'

MAURICE: 'There's more to this than meets the eye. Come on Aileen, let's get counting.'

They counted the twenty pound notes, piling them up in stacks of a thousand pounds. When they had finished, Maurice counted the stacks.

MAURICE: 'There is exactly one million pounds, and I would stake my life on it that they are all genuine.'

AILEEN: 'If it hasn't come from a burglary, where has it come from. Could it be a bank job?'

MAURICE: 'No. Banks don't keep this amount of cash these days. We only keep £25,000. Even Lloyds Bank would only keep £50,000. To get this amount of cash, you would have to request it and it would take a week. Somehow, I can't see our Irish and Australian burglars doing that.'

AILEEN: 'What do you suggest then?'

MAURICE: 'I suppose it could be a ransom, or blackmail. But why would they carry it round with them, knocking on doors, housebreaking. It doesn't make sense. If it wasn't so serious, I would say it was a practical joke.

AILEEN: 'Some joke! Who do you know that would joke with a million quid?'

MAURICE: 'Quite.'

AILEEN: 'So what do we do?'

MAURICE: 'Nothing. We'll put this suitcase away under the stairs and wait and see what happens. If our friendly door-to-door burglars turn up we can give them it back. It's not worth risking your life, even for a million pounds. But somehow, I don't think we will see them again.

So they packed the money back into the suitcase, put it at the back of the cupboard under the stairs, and covered it with an old coat.

Twenty-seven

Ruby got straight 'A's in her A levels. She was offered a place at Oxford to study History; a place at the Royal Academy of Music in London to study music; and a place at the Royal School of Art to study Art. If this weren't enough options, Lenny Ravowich rang her up offering to manage Ruby Kind professionally.

Ruby Kind were rehearsing in the barn. Ruby told them about Lenny's offer. They seemed uncharacteristically reticent. Ruby laughed at their worried faces. She knew the reason for it.

RUBY: 'Of course you must go to University. I may go myself if I can decide which one!'

There was a collective sigh of relief.

EVAN: 'We didn't know how to break it to you, Ruby. You've worked so hard with the band. We didn't want to seem ungrateful.'

RUBY: 'I didn't do it for you. I did it for me. Anyway, it wasn't hard work. I enjoyed doing it. I was going to thank you for all your hard work. We must keep in touch. Who knows, we may start up again after we have got our degrees. Which means that our next gig at school will be our swansong. Let's go out with a bang. Would you believe I have finally written a song. Have a listen to this and see what you think.'

Paolo had taken on a farm manager to look after the day to day running of the farm, leaving him free to concentrate on his horses, which he bred.

Jonah had bought out the other members of the Consortium who owned Tulip and transferred her to Paolo's stables. Paolo said she was a very beautiful horse. The ladies will love her. He would breed from her. Lucy came with Tulip. She too had noticed Paolo; Ruby had some competition.

Jonah was house hunting with Marie. Marie had two grown-up children, a boy, and a girl, who both lived in Rome. So Rome was the obvious place to look. Like Paolo, Jonah had let his farm to a tenant farmer.

Sophia was continuing with her medical studies, but she had bought a beautiful flat opposite the Spanish Steps.

As for Aileen and Maurice, they left the suitcase with the money in it under the stairs for a full six months. They didn't touch it. Eventually they decided to make a couple of test purchases with the cash. Maurice bought a shirt and Aileen bought a pair of shoes. They waited a couple of weeks. When nothing happened, they decided to buy something more expensive. They bought a double bed for £369. Maurice counted out the cash.

SALES ASSISTANT: 'Oh. You're paying cash! I can't remember the last time anyone paid in cash. People always use their cards these days.'

MAURICE: 'I know. I had a win at the races.'

SALES ASSISTANT: 'Did you indeed. Well done you. I like to go the races myself, but I usually lose. Not a lot. I'm not really a gambler; I just like to get dressed up.'

Can you give me any tips for the Ebor next week?'

MAURICE: 'No, sorry. I'm not really a gambler either. I just got lucky.'

Outside in Parliament Street, Aileen whispered urgently into Maurice's ear.

AILEEN: 'This can't go on, Maurice. People are suspicious when you pay in cash. We are just drawing attention to ourselves. I should know, I'm a shop manager for goodness sake.'

MAURICE: 'I know. I'll pay the money into our account at the building society.'

AILEEN: 'Won't your staff wonder where all that cash has come from?'

MAURICE: 'Not if I pay it in myself, when they have all gone home. I'll say I've got to work late. I do sometimes, you know.'

This placated Aileen, but Maurice knew it wasn't as simple as that. He would have to take at least one person into his confidence. When Mrs Bint retired, Maurice appointed Charlene Twopenny to the position of Chief Clerk. This aroused a good deal of resentment amongst the older women clerks. Charlene was only 24. The older women thought one of them should have been given the job as a reward for all of their years of hard work. But Charlene was a bright girl. She had a degree in Management Studies. Maurice could see in her the potential to become a Branch Manager with the Yorkshire Building Society. When he had to go away, she ran the office efficiently and dealt with the staff professionally. She didn't take any notice of them whispering behind her back.

The Building Society was open plan. But Maurice, as manager, had his own office.

MAURICE: 'When you have finished, Charlene, would you step into my office.'

CHARLENE: 'Yes, Sir.'

Ten minutes later there was a knock on the door and Charlene walked into Maurice's office.

MAURICE: 'Take a seat, Charlene. You've been Chief Clerk for what, six months now? How are you finding things?'

CHARLENE: 'Very good sir. I'm enjoying it.'

MAURICE: 'The others aren't giving you any bother are they?'

CHARLENE: 'No. I can handle them. I'm afraid I do sometimes wind them up.'

They both laughed at that.

MAURICE: 'I have a very delicate matter to deal with, Charlene. One that mustn't go beyond these four walls. Shall I continue or would you rather I didn't say any more?'

CHARLENE: 'I'm all ears.'

MAURICE: 'My wife has had a win on the lottery. She has won a million pounds.'

CHARLENE: 'But that's marvellous news. Why the long face?'

MAURICE: 'Aileen has done a silly thing. Heat of the moment, I suppose. She asked for the money to be paid in cash. She said she wanted to see what a million pounds looked like.'

CHARLENE: 'I can understand that.'

MAURICE: 'Can you? I'm not sure that I can. It's not safe to have a million pounds kicking about in your house. It needs to be in a bank or a building society, I'm going to pay the money into our account here at the building society,.'

CHARLENE: 'That will raise a few eyebrows with the geriatrics.'

Maurice laughed.

MAURICE: 'Is that what you call them: the geriatrics?'

CHARLENE: 'I do. They probably call me a lot worse.'

MAURICE: 'I had thought of that actually. I was going to wait until they had all gone home and then pay it in. But of course I'll need your help to do that, Charlene. If you agree, I'll fetch the money at lunchtime and we can book it in tonight.'

CHARLENE: 'Is that wise?'

MAURICE: 'The money is in a brand new suitcase. If anyone asks, I'll just say that I have bought a suitcase. But I don't expect them to ask.'

How did he do it? Maurice spread the money around his and Aileen's accounts, opened new accounts, and took out bonds. He made sure that the amount invested would not raise the interest of the Inland Revenue. Charlene asked if that was necessary. Mr Fish said that it was. Charlene accepted that; Mr Fish was the boss.

Aileen and Maurice bought a new car, a BMW 720. They took holidays in Australia, South Africa, Brazil. They both had good jobs so these things didn't look unusual to the neighbours, but they didn't tell anyone about the holiday home they bought in the Lake District.

Just about the whole of Joe Round's School had turned out for Ruby Kind's last gig. Ruby had invited Nathan, Lenny, and Miss Eyeball as well.

They sat at the back of the hall watching the young people. All three were impressed with how professional the band sounded now. They had come on leaps and bounds in the two years that they had been formed.

Ruby Kind were coming to the end of their set. Ruby spoke into the microphone.

RUBY: 'We'd like to end with a song that I have written myself. My thanks to Rod Stewart for the title: it's called 'Hot Legs.'

Ruby and Kirsty took the lead vocals.

HOT LEGS

Hot Legs it'll be alright,
looking like a switchblade on a motorbike
I'm a hot legs,
it'll be alright, going to the town tonight, alright
Headlight on a motorway, going pretty fast now,
there'll be hell to pay
Headlight on a motorway,
going to the town tonight, alright
Don't fail hear the sirens wail, going pretty fast now
they'll be on your tail
Don't fail hear the sirens wail,
going to the town tonight alright

Hot legs it'll be alright, looking like a switchblade on a motorbike
I'm a hot legs, it'll be alright, going to the town
Going to the town, going to the town tonight alright

NATHAN: 'Sign them up, Lenny. If that's not a hit, I'll eat my hat.'

LENNY: 'I'm trying. I'm trying.'

Ruby flew out to see Paolo. They were sat in the sunshine watching a new-born foal gambol about in the field, running around its mother. Ruby rested her head on Paulo's shoulder. He kissed her hair. All her life she had been looking for somewhere where she belonged, where she was wanted, where she was loved. It was better at Uncle Jonah's, but that was only ever going to be a marriage of convenience: it suited them both at the time, but that had gone now. Jonah was living with Marie in Rome. Had she found what she wanted here with Paolo, on his farm in Pisa? It certainly felt right at this moment. Jonah had written into the tenancy agreement that she could live at his farm as long as she wanted and have free use of the barn. She had met the new tenants. They were very nice, but she didn't think she would stay. It was time she spent some of Bruno's money and bought a place of her own. But that would depend on where she went to University. If she went to University.

Ruby loved Paolo and she was pretty sure that he loved her. What they needed was time. Time together. Maybe she should take a gap year and live here on the farm with Paolo.

RUBY: 'Paolo, can I stay here with you for a while?'

PAOLO: 'Of course. Stay as long as you want to … *'tesoro'* … stay until the mountains crumble into the sea.'

These last words he said in Italian, but Ruby knew what he meant.

At the fourth and final Mistie's auction of Bruno's house contents, the Petty Museum in California bought most of the paintings for £24 million. They had decided to hang onto the Leonardo da Vinci painting, as the auctioneer had advised.

The whole auction raised £32,126,247 after commission. Ruby, Jonah, Paolo and Sophia split it four ways.

Jonah and Ruby discussed making a return visit to Aileen as Mickey Mouse and Donald Duck, but decided against it. Even Aileen wouldn't fall for that again.

THE END

Also by Paul Philip Studer

SPUG
THE MAGIC PLANET

Paul Philip Studer

Tutuchamilabin or SPUG, as it is affectionately called - was a magic planet.

There were one hundred wizards who controlled its mystical lands. One of the wizards was called 'Thirty Seven', he was the Bonz's wizard. The Bonz were similar to an overgrown guinea pig, about a foot long and were governed by a King and Queen.

When the old king died, Bonz conundrums were held, to decide who should become the next King and Queen.

There was a part of SPUG where nobody ventured, on the map it said - 'There be dragons'. Wizard Zuron was determined to explore the area, when he did, he came face to face with Dragon Inferno and a tremendous battle took place.

SPUG – The Magic Planet

ISBN: 9781800947443

THE FRIVOLOUS CRIME SQUAD

Paul Philip Studer

It has always struck me as odd to have a police unit called The Serious Crime Squad. All crime is serious by definition. I know what they mean by 'Serious Crime: murder, rape, bank robbery, for example. 'Serious' is defined as:

> 1. Demanding or characterised by careful consideration or application.
> 2. Acting or speaking sincerely and in earnest, rather than in a joking or half-hearted manner.

You could apply that definition to investigating any crime. So, I have flipped it on its head - the opposite of serious is 'frivolous'. 'Frivolous' is defined as:

Not having any serious purpose or value.

I have invented crimes that the Serious Crime Squad would not touch:

> 1. Stealing collection money from a church.
> 2. Wheelie bin fire.
> 3. Theft of five pairs of very expensive knickers.

It follows therefore, that these crimes are frivolous; hence the name of the book!

The Frivolous Crime Squad

ISBN: 9781800947627

THE ADVENTURES OF VINNY

Paul Philip Studer

Vinny was a very streetwise cat - but one day, he forgot himself and caused the most horrendous car crash, involving multiple vehicles.

In the aftermath, the local Policeman - Sergeant Ventress, wants to have Vinny put to sleep, to ensure that he doesn't cause any further catastrophies. Unfortunately, no-one will tell the Sergeant where Vinny lives (they all know, but remain tight lipped)!

Other adventures include a very unpleasant journey to Whitby, spent under the bonnet of Elvis's delivery van. Another time, Vinny ends up in Aberdeen, stowed away in a removal van.

The Adventures of Vinny

ISBN: 9781800947924

THE Magic SLIPPERS

PAUL PHILIP STUDER

I was a casualty of my mother's ambition. My mother wanted me to do the same as my brother Anthony; he was a civil engineer.

Today was the day that the A level results would be posted on the school noticeboard.

I passed one A level: Maths - grade E. My parents went mad.

But I survived and went on to have a very good career in the building industry, as a planning surveyor.

Ironically my brother gave up his career in civil engineering and formed a company making kitchens.

The Magic Slippers
ISBN: 9781800947931

ESCAPE FROM MOSS PARK MENTAL HOSPITAL

a true story by
Paul Philip Studer

My wife, Diane, died on 3rd November 2022. We had been married 45 years. Her passing tipped me into a breakdown.

I went to Moss Park (mental health) Hospital as a voluntary patient, but they sent me to Scarborough, where I was sectioned. They should not have done that. It allowed them to keep me locked up for 6 months, which they did.

During that time, I was prevented from organising or even attending my own wife's funeral.

But, later, I escaped and went to Switzerland to search for my Swiss family. I didn't find them but my escape ultimately led to my release from hospital.

Escape from Moss Park Mental Hospital

ISBN: 9781800947993

PAUL PHILIP STUDER

Unit
TWO

Sequel to
THE MAGIC SLIPPERS

In this sequel to The Magic Slippers…

By a strange quirk of fate, Stu had found a job that he enjoyed and was good at. He was a Planning Surveyor responsible for drawing up programmes, material scheduling and measuring the bonus. He was the Site Manager's right-hand man and even ran sites himself when the need arose.

Stu was in a construction unit called Unit Two: a great bunch of lads, always up for a laugh, especially with their Tea Lady, Mavis. She ended up subjected to exploding cigarettes and purple tea. Jack Wild was the Construction Manager. He ended up the victim of exploding caps under his blotter and taped to the wheels of his chair.

The biggest challenge for Stu was the job at the Film, Photography and Television Museum in Bradford. Stu ran it himself and it tested him to the limit.

Unit Two

ISBN: 9781800948129

PAUL PHILIP STUDER

LOVE LUCY

Three generations of Charleston Monrow's family had been killed in a car crash. They had been on their way to see him at Oxford University. It had a catastrophic effect on Charleston; he barely scraped through his degree in English.

He had been offered a job at the Daily Mail but it was dependent upon him getting a first class degree. When he achieved only a third class, Bent Boghammer IV, editor of the Daily Mail, said he wouldn't wipe his ass on a third class degree.

As events transpired, Charleston and his girlfriend, Lucy, end up as roadies in Australia, working for a band called The Drumbeats. They were very big down under.

Some of the equipment was damaged in the sea voyage to Australia. Charleston, a whizz with electronics, managed to repair the equipment and the band played to a sell-out concert at the Sydney Opera House.

Love Lucy

ISBN: 9781800948303

BLUE
EYES
PAUL PHILIP STUDER

Sam and Dennis were planning a trip into the bush, only this time they were taking a gas ring and a gas bottle to cook on. Last time they had tried to do it the Aborigine way and light a fire with twigs, but they couldn't find enough twigs to light the fire. They didn't have enough money to buy a gas bottle, so they borrowed old Ma Hutchins' gas bottle. She had died at Christmas.

Unable to carry the heavy gas bottle home, they stashed it underneath the schoolhouse, planning to pick it up tomorrow morning with the trailer. Sam and Dennis didn't know it, but the gas bottle was leaking.

Eamonn was caretaker at the school in Crocodile Bay. He was a lifelong smoker. He lit a cigarette and took a long drag. When he finished, he discarded the cigarette butt under the schoolhouse. There was a loud explosion heard for miles around and the little wooden schoolhouse disappeared from town.

It should have been a disaster, but everyone survived. Only moments after the ambulance arrived, a little girl of five was found unconscious…

Blue Eyes

ISBN: 9781800948464

PAUL PHILIP STUDER

GOING HOME

A large van turned into Thirsk High Street. From nowhere, a pig ran out across the road right in front of the van. Alo, the driver swerved to avoid the pig. The van tipped onto its side and crashed into the Nationwide Building Society.

Alo ended up in hospital with a broken leg, a broken arm and a bandaged head. Lucy wrote to Alo's mum and dad in the Grand Canyon. Alo's mum wrote to him in hospital telling him to come home and that she would look after him. He hadn't been home since he was 17 years old, when he'd left in the middle of the night to join the festival circuit.

Alo has a girlfriend called Irene Burns, Managing Director of Burns Construction. She flies out to see him in the Grand Canyon. She hires a Learjet for the trip. Irene never thought she would marry: she was married to her job. But leaving Alo to go back to work on Monday was becoming increasingly difficult. Maybe the impossible was going to happen. Maybe she would marry Alo.

Going Home
ISBN: 9781800948631

*Available worldwide from Amazon
and all good bookstores*

Michael Terence
Publishing

www.mtp.agency

mtp.agency

@mtp_agency*

Milton Keynes UK
Ingram Content Group UK Ltd.
UKHW031155251124
451529UK00001B/21